a hundred ways to
LOVE

OTHER TITLES BY ELLIE WADE

Forever Baby
Fragment
Chasing Memories
A Hundred Ways to Love

THE CHOICES SERIES

A Beautiful Kind of Love
A Forever Kind of Love
A Grateful Kind of Love

THE FLAWED HEART SERIES

Finding London
Keeping London
Loving London
Eternally London
Taming Georgia (Stand-Alone Spin-Off)

PLEASE VISIT ELLIE'S AMAZON AUTHOR PAGE AT
HTTP://AMZN.TO/2CCXIVN FOR MORE INFORMATION
ON HER OTHER BOOKS.

WOULD YOU LIKE TO KNOW WHEN ELLIE HAS
GIVEAWAYS, SALES, OR NEW RELEASES?

SIGN UP FOR HER NEWSLETTER AT
WWW.ELLIEWADE.COM. ♥

a hundred ways to LOVE

ELLIE WADE

ISBN-13: 978-1-944495-10-7

For Kylie, I love you, girl!
You are such a beautiful person inside and out.
I'm so grateful to call you a friend.
Can't wait to hug you in real life someday soon.
Thanks for loving Leni. ♥

prologue

Leni
Age Thirteen

The mound of clay spins on the pottery wheel before me. My hands, the color of mud, rest atop the blurry blob as it turns. I blink hard and pull in a deep breath, willing the emotions that threaten to spill from my eyes to stay away. I won't cry because of him. I'd never give him that satisfaction.

Yet the truth is that my back aches tremendously. Every movement of my arm causes a shooting pain to run down my back, the worst of the agony centered on the area where it hit the corner of his mahogany desk. I've seen my father hit my mother before, but he's never physically hurt me. I knew the second the words left my mouth, the moment his eyes widened with fury, that there would be severe consequences.

"I don't care that some jerk's daughter is going to attend the summer camp. If you can't make friends with that snob on your own, that's your problem. I'm not going to suck up to his daughter, so he'll be your friend. There's nothing you can do to make me."

The entire encounter probably lasted a matter of seconds, but I saw it all in slow motion. His fists clenched at his sides, his knee bent up, rising toward his waist, before his hideous, overpriced alligator-skinned loafer shot toward my chest with a wrath I knew to fear. I didn't feel the initial blow as it lifted my body off of the ground, propelling me through the air. The pain of the impact against his desk blinded me, stealing the air from my lungs.

It wasn't until I hit the ground and could breathe again that I truly felt the pain. I couldn't have contained the agony if I'd wanted to. It broke out of me in sob-filled screams that mimicked a wounded animal, not me.

But it was me.

The cries of pain came from my quivering lips as tears rolled down my cheeks and onto the floor. When I was strong enough to stand, he was no longer in his office with me.

I was alone, but I'm no stranger to solitude. Besides the three months each year I get to spend at my grandmother's, I crave it.

It's always just me and my art, which I suppose is my own personal therapy. Living in this house with my parents is a nightmare. But, through my creative expression, I'm able to find a semblance of peace, enough to get me through the school year until I can see Mimi and my best friend, Liam, again.

They say that what doesn't kill you makes you stronger, and I believe it. Growing up in this house with these people has been molding me into the fiercest woman to ever live. I will never be like my parents. I will never settle for less than I deserve. I will give up anything to make it. No cost is too great to stop me from breaking free.

It sucks to wish your childhood away, but that's the hand I've been dealt. Some have better childhoods than me; some have it worse. It is what it is. I can drown in the sorrow, or I can fight.

I've been a fighter since the day I was born.

My parents have tried to shape me into someone I'm not my entire life but with no success. As the years go by, their attempts grow, but so does my resolve. I'm as stubborn and strong-willed as they come, and perhaps that's the reason I'm able to hold on to who I want to be and not change into the daughter they'd prefer.

The daughter they wish they had would've gladly fluttered off to the equestrian camp to schmooze with the spoiled daughter of Dad's business associate. But I'm going to Mimi's. There's not anything they can do to stop me from spending my summers at the farm of the only person who really loves me, where I get to hang out with my only real friend, Liam.

I wince as my hands work the clay. It hurts my bruised muscles but not as much as not doing it would hurt my broken soul. The earthen material spins faster, smoothing out with my touch. Calm takes over as I think of nothing. Peace fills me as my hands create of their own accord.

I smile when Mimi and Liam take hold of my thoughts. In just over two weeks, I'll be there. I love everything about Mimi, but mainly, I'm grateful for her unconditional love. I enjoy every adventure that Liam and

I share. Most of all, I'm thankful that he accepts me for me.

In five fleeting years, I can leave this house for good. And I'll never have to come back.

I startle as the door to the spare room that I've turned into my art studio slams open with a loud thud.

"All of it, gone." My father's gruff voice directs two men.

It takes a moment for me to grasp the reality of what's happening. I gasp. "No!" I shout at the strangers as they start tossing my finished canvases into large garbage bags. "Stop!" I scream, jumping up from the stool.

My clay-covered hands pull at a canvas he's attempting to throw out but to no avail. He snatches it from my grasp and continues his destruction.

"What are you doing?" I yell at my father.

He ignores me, his arms crossed over his chest with a smug smile present on his perfectly shaved face.

"Stop this!" I scream as I watch all of my supplies being tossed away.

My father turns to me and very calmly states, "Your actions have consequences, Eleanora. You'd be wise to remember that."

My mind races. "Fine. Just stop them, please," I plead.

He clears his throat. "I've indulged this little hobby of yours for too long as it is. It's time you grow up some and learn some respect."

Tears blur my vision as I watch all my treasures being thrown out, incapable of stopping it. Hate festers beneath my skin, and I swear to myself that I will never speak to this man again once I'm out of this house.

"I hate you," I say under my breath.

He doesn't respond, but I know he heard me.

Five more years.

The men leave, bags in hand. I'm left standing in the one place here that made me happy. Everything I loved about it was just ripped from me.

"You will be attending that camp this summer," he snaps before turning and walking out.

My knees buckle, and I fall onto the floor in a mass of tears. I try to be strong and not let my parents dictate my happiness. I try to be fearless, but in this moment, I feel that I'm losing. A summer filled with no art, no Mimi's, and a stay at Snobs R Us camp ... I can't. It will break me.

I lie on the floor of the empty room until I can't cry anymore. Staring at the ceiling, I feel sorry for myself for just a few minutes.

Enough.

I hold on to the table, using it to help me get up. By the time I'm standing, all the self-pity is replaced with determination. My father needs to realize that, when it comes to me, he'll never win.

My mom comes into the vacant room to tell me that it's time for dinner.

"I'm going to Mimi's when school is out in two weeks," I firmly tell her. "You'd better talk to Dad and make that happen because, if you don't, everyone will know the type of person he really is. I've taken pictures of the bruises all over my back, and I will tell everyone what he did, including the authorities. I will send a letter to every person you know, making sure that they all know what being the daughter of Henry and Eleanora Turner is really like. I will not stop until I ruin his reputation. Do you understand?"

My mother's eyes are wide, a bewildered confusion evident on her face. She simply nods and leaves the room.

I haven't taken pictures of my back, but that's not the point. There's nothing that my parents value more than their reputation in their social circle. My mother never stands up to my father, but she'll find a way to protect him from this.

I know he'll make the next five years a living hell for me, but as long as I have my summers with Mimi, I can get through anything.

one

Leni

If my mother were here, she would tell me that my eyes were going to get stuck in the back of my head with the amount of eye-rolling that I was doing. Yet my mother wouldn't be caught dead on a stinky Greyhound bus, so my eyes are free to roll at will.

I lean back into my seat. My head rests against the questionable blue upholstered seat, and I try not to let my mind wander to all the germs that are surely embedded in each thread of the chair cover. I've never been a fan of public transportation despite the years I've used it.

Holding my phone up, I continue to scroll through my Instagram feed. It makes me literally nauseous. Post after post of my friends in New York City, enjoying their Saturday night in "the greatest place on earth." They all have appropriate hashtags to put emphasis on the pure amazingness of their lives.

#blessed

#bestlife
#lucky
#sohappy
#pinchmeImustbedreaming
#bestboyfriendever

Seriously, Madison? Best boyfriend ever? Totally #stfu. I'm glad that silver Tiffany necklace that you just posted eighty-five pictures of erases the last year of Stewart screwing other skanks behind your back.

"Ugh," I grumble under my breath.

Social media is killing America, and if not America, then my soul—at the very least. Facebook and Instagram posts are the fleeting moments of happiness in someone's mediocre, if not completely lame-ass, day.

Am I jealous?

Hell yeah, I'm turning green from envy. I want to be #blessed in #nyc. But I'm a #loser on the way to #loserville to live with my grandma. How does one spell despair? That's simple—T-E-X-A-S. I'm being a brat; I know it. Elkwood is actually a sweet little Texas town that holds the best memories from my otherwise depressing childhood.

My summers spent with my grandmother, Mary Turner, whom I lovingly refer to as Mimi, are true highlights of my life. If it were a thing back then, every moment in Elkwood would have been social media–worthy.

Just going back there now means that I've failed. Just as my father said I would.

When I left Texas five years ago, I had no intention of going back.

After high school, everything was falling into place. I had been accepted into Cooper Union, home to one of the most prestigious undergrad art programs in the nation. Major bonus points that the college of my dreams was located in the most magnificent city in the world—New York City. I was going to attend college, refine my art skills, graduate, and create beautiful pieces that people from all over the world would clamor to buy. I would most likely meet and marry another artist, and the two of us would spend the rest of our days doing what we loved.

It was *the dream*.

Yet it wasn't my father's.

My father has always been a difficult man for me to connect with. The only thing bigger than his ego is his ambition. He had no desire to take over his father's farm. The second he could, he left for Houston and began pursuing his political career. He's always wanted to be a man of stature, of power. He's now a Texas senator, and if he has his way, I'm sure he'll run for president at some point.

My mom is the polar opposite of my father. She has no need for personal glory. Her only ambition seems to be helping my father with his.

I am the only child of Henry and Eleanora Turner, who have had my entire life planned out from the moment I was born. The only problem is that I've never been who they want me to be. I'm no debutant. When I refused to pursue a "respectable" degree, such as political science or business, my father cut me off. In fact, besides the few Christmas presents my mom sends me each year, I've received nothing from my parents since I left their home in Highland Park, Texas five years ago.

Unfortunately, it seems a hundred twenty thousand dollars in student loan debt and an art degree leaves one with very few options. For the past year since graduating, I've been working my ass off. Despite having two jobs and three roommates in an apartment the size of my parents' kitchen, I couldn't make it in New York. I spent more on art supplies than I ever made in sales. I ended up giving away most of my pieces.

Mimi sent me enough money to buy a one-way bus ticket to Elkwood. So, here I am, forced to sit on this bus for two days, with nothing more to do than think about my life and the mess that it is. I've lost my cool New York apartment, my group of hip and eclectic friends, my art, and the dream I had for my life. All my worldly possessions fit into one suitcase, and the sad part is, there's room to spare. I can't even stuff a suitcase.

Pathetic.

I'm left staring at other people's lives on a phone that's going to shut off at any minute since the bill hasn't been paid in a couple of months.

#lifeisgrand

I want to cry.

Despite my better judgment, I continue to scroll through social media until the battery on my phone dies. I throw the phone in my purse with a sigh.

Pulling my knees up, I rest them against the seat in front of me and lean my head against the window. As far as the eye can see, there are fields of tan grass. I'm not sure where we are. I just hope the rest of this ride passes quickly.

Sadly, New York was never meant to be. That's my reality. Elkwood isn't my end destination either, but I'm anxious to get there, so I can start figuring out a plan to get to where I'm supposed to be.

A day of self-pity and insane jealousy catches up to me, and my eyelids become heavy. The soothing motion of the moving bus, the low rumble of its engine, and the exhaustion that pure heartbreak brings pull me into sleep. Right before slumber takes me, I see my sweet Mimi, and my heart smiles. In a world where I feel I've lost everything, I still have her unconditional love, and right now, that has to be enough.

I bolt awake. Passengers are filing down the aisle of the bus, bags in hand. Looking out the window, I see the Elkwood bus station.

We're here!

My past woes are momentarily forgotten as my excitement to see Mimi grows. I pull out my phone to call her, only to remember that it's dead.

Hmm.

I try to recall where I left my charger. I'll have to plug my phone in for a minute somewhere around the bus station, so I can call Mimi to come get me.

I exit the bus and retrieve my single suitcase. After an extensive search through my purse and luggage for my charger, I come up, hands empty. Darn, I'm sure it's right where I left it—plugged into the wall back in my New York apartment.

The sad thing is that I don't even know her phone number by heart, or I would just ask to borrow someone's phone. She's number one on my speed dial, but that's of little help with a dead phone. I don't think a town as small as Elkwood has Uber or taxis—not that I have any money to pay for a ride anyway. I left when I literally had nothing.

I start walking, pulling my suitcase behind me. Mimi's farm is a few miles outside of town, I think. I guess I've never really thought about it. Yet it shouldn't take me more than a couple of hours to walk it.

I hope.

I'm so hungry that I could eat my hand, and I finished off my last granola bar on the bus. My mind drifts to dreams of Mimi's homemade bread with real butter and jam.

Oh, jam. Maybe she'll have raspberry—my favorite.

I moan, not caring who hears me because I would do anything for a piece of that bread right now.

When's the last time I ate bread? Wow, I don't even know.

Over the past five years, bread slowly got replaced with salad greens. PB & J sandwiches were replaced with sushi and mac and cheese with brown rice. Come to think of it, I don't know how or why it happened. It just did. Comfort foods weren't in style with the crowd I hung out with. I suppose that's healthier, but now that I really think about it, it's weird.

Seriously, when was the last time I ate a piece of bread? This is going to bother me.

My thoughts are pulled from the soft deliciousness of Mimi's bread to the squeal of tires. I turn to the side to see headlights from a large truck barreling toward me, mere inches from my face.

Well, crap.

I didn't think my life could get worse, but I underestimated the wrath of the universe. They say that, the moment before you die, your entire life flashes before your eyes. The split second before my death isn't that way. As I close my eyes and brace for impact, my thoughts aren't of my family, my joys, or my regrets. My focus is singular.

Now, I'm never going to get another piece of Mimi's bread. This sucks.

two

Liam

"Holy shit!" I yell out as I slam my foot against the brakes as hard as I can. My hands clench around the steering wheel, my knuckles strained white with fear-gripped anticipation of the horrible thud to come.

I'm propelled forward, and my chest hits my seat belt, sending me back into the seat. The truck has come to a complete stop. I don't loosen my desperate grip on the steering wheel as I cautiously look out the windshield.

Inches away from the front end of my truck is a woman. She's standing, untouched.

Oh, thank you.

I say a prayer of gratitude as I swing the door open and jump out of the truck.

My gratitude turns to anger as the thought dawns on me that I could have killed this chick because she decided to step in front of a moving vehicle.

"What the hell? Are you okay?" I say to her as I round the front of my truck.

She opens her eyes wide, and the next angry question I was going to shout out gets lodged in my throat because I know those big green eyes. I'd know them anywhere.

"Eleanora?"

This seems to snap her out of her state of shock.

"William," she scoffs, her beautiful greens squinting in anger, as she uses my formal name as if we were nothing more than mere acquaintances.

"It's Liam," I answer her like I always do.

"Yeah, well, you know damn well that it's Leni. What are we, seven years old again?"

"Yeah, I knew a Leni," I admit, "but I lost her years ago." I hate that my voice comes out thick with emotion, but when it comes to Leni, I can't help it.

She rolls her eyes and begins to stomp the rest of the way across the road.

"Wait! Leni, stop."

God, this woman drives me insane.

Woman? I suppose she is.

The last time I saw Leni, she was sixteen. I guess she's twenty-three now. I'd be lying if I said that I hadn't thought about her a little too much over the years. Despite her irrational and inexplicable hatred toward me, I've always found her insanely gorgeous.

She no longer wears her little pixie cut that she insisted on in her preteen years despite her mother's pleas to let it grow. Her chocolate-brown locks fall in waves down the center of her back. Her nose and the tops of her cheeks are still spattered with light freckles that have always turned me on way more than they should have. And yet the part of her that has always gotten me is her eyes. They're a deep emerald green, and I can't describe them any other way but to say that they almost sparkle—usually with rage when they're directed my way but a sparkle just the same.

"What do you want, *Liam*?" she says with a sigh as she turns toward me.

"Was that hard to say?" I smirk, knowing she wants to call me by my formal first name, just as I want to call her by hers. It's always been a tool of ours, a surefire way to piss the other one off.

"Yeah, it was."

"Well, I want to know why you just walked in front of my truck." Anger builds as I remember what just happened. "I could've killed you."

She rolls her eyes. "I didn't mean to walk in front of you. I was thinking about stuff and clearly wasn't watching my surroundings. I'm just tired. Thank you for not killing me." She turns and starts to walk away from me.

"Wait!"

"What?" she snaps.

"What are you doing here?" My attention falls to the large bag she's pulling behind her.

"I'm going to Mimi's."

"Do you want a ride?"

She shrugs. "No, it's fine. I can walk."

"You're going to walk to the farm?" I ask slowly.

"Yeah," she says with a nod, as if it's not a big deal.

"That's stupid, Leni. Let me drop you off. I'm obviously going that way."

She shakes her head. "I'm fine with walking."

I just want to scream at her. *How can she still be so stubborn after all these years?*

"Get in the truck!" I yell at her.

"No!" she yells back.

15

"Damn it, Leni! Get in the truck! You can't even walk across the street without almost getting hit. How are you going to walk five miles to the farm? What would I tell your grandmother if you got plowed over by someone else?" I grab the handle of her bag and yank it from her grasp. I throw it in the back of my truck. "I would've thought you'd grown up some in the big city. Evidently, you haven't."

She huffs as she climbs up into the passenger seat and slams the door closed. She crosses her arms across her chest. "Well, I can assure you that you wouldn't know anything about that since you've never left this town. It's hard to gauge appropriate human behavior since you only communicate with cows."

The second her seat belt is fastened, I hit the gas and peel out down the street. I can't wait to drop her off.

"Well, actually, I went to college for four years, so I have left this town. And I can assure you, I understand people just fine. Like, for instance, I can see perfectly clear that you've grown up to be a pretentious, judgmental witch, just like your mother."

She gasps. "I am nothing like my mother!"

I chuckle. "Really? Have you looked in the mirror lately?"

I'm ashamed of myself that I've stooped to her immaturity level. I should have never brought her mother into this. I know how much animosity exists between those two. Leni just makes me so insane with fury. I used to try so hard to be her friend, and she's always pushed me away.

She doesn't have a rebuttal. I've silenced the girl who never shuts up, and I feel like an ass.

"I didn't mean that. I'm sorry."

"Yeah, you did." is her only reply as she continues to stare out the window.

"Len, I'm sorry. I truly am. That was a shitty thing to say. I just don't know why we're still fighting. We're adults. It doesn't have to be like this."

She turns her head toward me, and I'm expecting anger, but in her eyes, I see something else. It seems that she's looking to me with a sense of longing mixed with some sadness, but before I can be sure, she faces the window once more.

I think back to when we were really young. I met Leni when I was six. She's only a year younger than me, but she seemed so much smaller. I called her the girl with lucky eyes because they were the color of a four-leaf clover. Leni's grandparents' ranch and my parents' ranch shared a border, and I spent my time in between them. Invisible borders weren't taken into account when I was discovering new lands on my adventures. Leni's grandparents didn't care if I was on their land anyway. I first met her when she was playing in the rows of corn during one of her summer visits. At six years old, I considered her my best friend. We played every day that summer and every summer after that until the summer of my fourteenth birthday. She turned into quite the brat that year, and it only got worse.

I tried to remain friends with her, but she wasn't enjoyable to be around. I went over to see her when she arrived the summer of my seventeenth birthday. It was a mistake, and I stopped trying after that. I was busy helping my dad with the cattle and crops. I didn't have time for Leni's juvenile games.

Yet I'd be lying if I said that I didn't look toward her grandma's house every time I passed it over the past seven years, hoping that Leni might be there and that I'd get to see a glimpse of her even if just for a second.

I guess you never forget your first love even if I didn't realize back then that was what she was.

"So, how long are you in town?" I attempt to lighten the heavy mood.

"Not sure. Hopefully, not long."

"Well, it's nice to see you. You look good." The last statement is a gross understatement. She doesn't look good; she looks incredible.

"Okay," she scoffs with an edge to her voice.

I grip the steering wheel tighter and close my mouth shut. My chest feels heavy in a way I can't fully comprehend. We're exactly where we left off the summer of my seventeenth birthday.

I'm relieved when we finally arrive. I park my truck in front of the barn and turn off the engine.

"I can walk in by myself. You're free to go," Leni says as she hops out of my truck.

After exiting the truck, I lift her suitcase from the back and set it down on the ground.

"Okay, thanks. But I have some work to take care of in the barn," I force myself to say without attitude.

She walks around the truck and grabs ahold of her suitcase handle. "Why are you doing work in Mimi's barn?"

"Because it's my barn."

"What does that mean?" she quips.

I look to her in question. *Does she not know?*

"You know I bought your grandma's farm, right?"

"What?" She asks, dropping her bags on the gravel driveway.

"I bought the farm," I slowly tell her again.

"When? Why?" she shrieks, her eyes bulging with panic.

"Um, a couple of years ago now, I guess. Because it was for sale, and it's right next to my dad's land. So, it just made sense to expand our ranch."

"Why would Mimi sell her land? Where is she living? So, you just kicked her out on the streets? Why would you do this to her? She's been nothing but kind to you your whole life!" Leni's eyes are brimming with tears.

I raise my hands in an attempt to calm her. "Shh. No, it's not like that. I didn't kick her out, Len. She's free to stay in her house for as long as she wants. I'm just farming the land, is all."

I don't know if Leni heard a word I said. She just looks to me with so much loathing.

"I can't believe you did this, William Moore." She shakes her head as a tear rolls down her cheek.

I reach out my arm to grab hers, but she bolts off toward the house before I can.

I'm left here, watching her run away from me again. And, just like when I was a teenager, I have no idea why she harbors such disgust—and, worse yet, why it bothers me so much.

Three

Leni

I sprint toward the old farmhouse, leaving my belongings by the truck.

I can't believe Mimi sold everything!

I'm across the front porch in two strides and swinging the front door open.

"Mimi!" I shriek when I enter the house.

My grandma comes hastily out of the kitchen, wiping her hands on her apron, a look of concern spread across her face.

My tears flow harder because she's aged so much in the five years since I last saw her. She has more wrinkles than she's ever had and looks tired.

Why haven't I come to see her in five years?

The guilt weighs down on me as my panic rises.

She wraps her arms around me, and I melt into her embrace as sobs rack my body. She leads us over to the sofa, and I continue to cry as she holds me.

My emotions are playing a game of ping-pong on my heart, and they're still not enough for me to even pinpoint why I'm so upset, but I am. I'm devastated.

And it's not just one thing either; it's so many, and maybe that's why I can't focus on a single cause.

A loving hand continues to rub my back, but the tears won't abate. I'm so broken. I've lost everything I've ever wanted. The dream I'd had for my life died the moment I stepped on that bus. There's so much guilt.

How could I not know that my grandmother sold her life's work, her legacy? Why haven't I been back to see her?

There was always an excuse as to why—work, money, homework, bills, commitments. The list was vast, five years of excuses.

I'm no better than my parents. Liam is right. I'm a horrible person.

Speaking of Liam, seeing him again caused so much emotion to well up inside me—most of which, I can't name. His presence made me uneasy, and I can't figure it out.

Eventually, my tears run dry, and I pull my wet face away from Mimi's chest. She smiles at me and wipes my face with her apron.

"I'm so sorry," I choke out.

"Shh … don't you worry yourself, baby girl."

Her smile has always made me feel so loved.

"Why did you sell the farm? Why would you do that? Why didn't Dad help you if you needed money? I don't understand what's going on." I attempt to remain calm.

"Oh, my Leni girl." She swipes a lock of my hair behind my ear. "You're tired. You've had a long couple of days. All this can wait. First, you need to eat." She pats her lap and stands.

"But, Mimi—"

"It can wait, dear. I just pulled some bread out of the oven. Would you like a slice or two while I finish up dinner?" She walks into the kitchen.

OMG … bread.

"Do you have jam?" I sniffle.

"How about some raspberry?" she asks while surveying the contents of the refrigerator.

"Yes!" I all but scream, making my grandma laugh.

She has the best laugh. Always has.

After I've stuffed a few pieces of warm amazingness in my mouth, I feel like a different person.

"Feel better?" Mimi asks.

"So much better," I say through a mouthful of bread. Looking down at the plate before me, I see that I've almost polished off the entire loaf by myself.

"Life's woes are always worse when we're hungry."

"I was so hungry," I admit.

She sets a glass of milk down on the table and takes my chin in her hand, looking me in the eyes. "I'm glad you're back. I know it's not what you wanted, but I can't tell you how happy I am to see you."

"I'm happy to see you, too. I'm so sorry I didn't come back to visit." My bottom lip begins to tremble.

"No more of that." She pats my knee before heading back over toward the stove. "You were living your life, dear. There's nothing to apologize for. I've lived a great life, and I want that for you." She pulls a chicken leg out of the bubbling oil and places it on a paper towel. "Plus, you called me every week."

"I know, but that's not the same as seeing you. I'm sorry."

She finishes pulling the rest of the fried chicken out of the pan and brings the dishes of food to the table.

She's made all my favorites—fried chicken, homemade mac and cheese, rice, and gravy.

"Mimi, you didn't have to do all this." I shake my head at the impressive spread before me.

"I wanted to. It's not every day that my Leni girl comes back to me. You deserve a suitable homecoming meal."

"This is way more food than the two of us can possibly eat." I chuckle.

"You know me. I can never make proper portions." Mimi lets out a laugh.

"So, please tell me about the farm. Why is that jerk out in your barn?" My insides twist up, and I feel my anger rising again, just thinking about Liam.

"You mean, Liam? Oh, honey, he's no jerk. He might be the sweetest man in Elkwood, to be honest. I know you can't remember your grandpa very well." She looks past me with a serene smile on her face, no doubt thinking about my pops who passed away when I was six.

She continues, "But your grandpa was smart. He was a great rancher and businessman. When he passed, he left me with a sizeable savings to keep the ranch running. Unfortunately, he never really taught me how to do it all. Perhaps I should have asked for help. But you know me. I'm a hardheaded ole broad. There's nothing I can't do."

She grins toward me, and I know she's thinking that I'm just like her. She's told me many times that I remind her of herself, and that thought makes me proud.

"So, I did it my way. I hired help and bought and sold livestock and crops as best I could. Yet, every year, I'd end in the red, and I'd have to dip into my savings to balance the books. Well, after fifteen years of this, that money ran out. Truthfully, Leni, I was going to lose the farm. I had nothing left. I started inquiring around on the best way to sell it off, and Liam made me an offer." She points her finger in my direction. "And I'll tell you, it was more generous than it should have been. I told him as much, but he wouldn't hear it. He bought my land for more than anyone else would have. Then, to top it off, he insisted I stay in my house. He won't even accept rent. That boy saved me, Leni. He saved me." Her voice trails off.

"Why didn't you ask Dad for help? You know he has the money."

"Oh, my son has left me and this life behind. It's unfortunate, but it's the way it is. He's never wanted anything to do with this farm. I'll always love your father, Leni; he's my only son, but he didn't grow into a good man. Call it pride or stubbornness, but I couldn't reach out to him. I just couldn't do it." She shakes her head.

"I know what you mean," I say with a sigh. "I'd never ask my father for help either. Why didn't you tell me about the farm? That you were in trouble and had to sell? You never mentioned it." My voice lowers with the last sentence. Hurt permeates my chest. I press my palm against it just to ease the pain.

"Oh, baby girl." Mimi dismissively waves her hand out. "Why? There wasn't anything you could've done about my financial situation. It would've just made you sad for me. I didn't want you to worry when you were so far away. I wanted you to focus on your schooling."

I take in Mimi's words, and I know she's right. It would've devastated me, and unfortunately, there wouldn't have been anything I could've done. Renewed anger fills me as I think of my father and the fact that he could've helped if he'd bothered to check in on his mother even once in the past several years.

"You know, Dad, he was right about me though. I've failed, Mimi. I went to an amazing school and lived in one of the greatest cities for art in the world, and I couldn't make it."

"Oh, heavens. You are not a failure, not in the least. You had a dream, and you went for it. That, my girl, already makes you a success. *Making it* is subjective. What does that even look like? There are countless ways in which you can gauge your success. You know what I say? I say, if you get to wake up every day and do what you love, then you're living your best life. That's all any of us can do. There's no reason you can't work on your pretty pieces here, now is there?"

For the first time in recent history, I feel like I can breathe again.

I've been suffocating for so long.

I find myself in this place where I've done everything I vowed to my younger self that I would do. I checked all the boxes.

Leave Texas. Check.

Incredible art school. Check.

Guard my heart and protect myself. Check.

I had a plan, and I followed it. I left the person I love most in this world, Mimi, and lost my best friend, Liam, in the process. Yet I still did it, so I wouldn't lose myself. I fought to be independent. I worked hard and made ends meet despite all the odds stacked against me. I went weeks on end of eating just one meal a day. I saved pennies to buy toilet paper from the dollar store. I always worked multiple jobs, prioritizing work over sleep. It was a nightmare at times, but it was my dream, and I was reaching it.

And I did. I finished school.

I fought so hard, and I failed nonetheless. A degree alone doesn't make one successful. I would know; I'm the poster child for that campaign.

My father hasn't been present in my life for years now, and yet his darkness still pulls me down. I've reached every objective I set for myself yet accomplished nothing. Now, I'm back, and I have no idea what to do. I've been following my plan up until this point, but it didn't have the results I needed. So, what now? I have no clue where to begin or how to pull myself from this depression that's pulled me under. I'm lower than I've ever been. Thanks to Mimi, I can breathe, but life is more than that basic life function—so much more. Right now, that's all I have.

There's a knock on the front door. My head snaps toward it.

"I'll get it." My grandma gently taps my hand before leaving the table.

As soon as she opens the door, I hear Liam say, "Ma'am, Leni left her belongings out by my truck. I wanted to make sure they made it inside before I left for the night."

"That is very sweet of you, Liam. Thank you. Just set them in here."

Liam brings my purse and suitcase in the house. I try not to look at him, but honestly, I'm unable to stop myself. He's evidently been doing something strenuous because his shirt is damp with sweat. And his hair is all wet and disheveled and extremely sexy.

Wait, what? Where did that thought come from?

I suppose, regardless of who he is, I'd be lying if I didn't acknowledge—if just to myself—that he was quite beautiful in a manly kind of way.

Thinking back, I suppose he has always been good-looking. He used to have that boy-next-door thing going for him with his broad smile, perfect teeth, kind brown eyes, and that type of hair where you don't know if it should be described as blond or brown. In the bright Texas sun, it is blond, but right now, it's darker. And did I mention ... it's wet?

What the hell was he doing out there?

He's so different than anyone I found attractive in New York. Most of the guys I dated wore skinny jeans and form-fitting shirts, and their biceps were probably smaller than Liam's forearm. They would have looked ridiculous in a pair of Wranglers and cowboy boots, just as Liam would never be able to pull off skinny jeans.

I'm startled from my secret Liam thoughts when I hear my grandma ask Liam to join us for dinner.

"Oh, no, thank you, ma'am. I appreciate the offer, but I should get home and get cleaned up. I'm not fit as company right now."

"Nonsense!" Mimi chirps happily. "I've made enough food to feed an army; you'd be doing me a favor. Please stay."

"All right. Thank you, ma'am. I'll just go get washed up really quick." Liam goes into the bathroom.

As soon as the door closes behind him, I whisper-yell, "Why did you invite him in? It's going to be so awkward, Mimi!"

"Oh, stop." She nonchalantly waves me off. "You two used to be great friends. It will do you some good to catch up for a bit."

"We're not friends now. It won't be great at all ... just uncomfortable."

"Why aren't you friends again? I never understood what happened. One minute, you two were inseparable, and the next, you hated him."

"I have no idea," I grumble. "Truthfully, I don't know. I just know that I don't like him. I don't *need* him as a friend, Mimi."

"Oh, Leni girl … I swear, you're your own worst enemy sometimes."

"What does that mean?" I ask as Liam exits the bathroom. I shoot my grandma a look, letting her know that she doesn't need to answer right now.

Liam sits down at the table and starts dishing up.

"So, how was it that you and Leni crossed paths today? We haven't gotten to that story yet," Mimi asks Liam.

Liam starts to tell Mimi about me walking into the road and him almost plowing me over.

Mimi gasps. "You were supposed to call me when you got in."

"My phone died, and I forgot my charger," I say by way of explanation.

"Thank you for bringing her back," Mimi says to Liam.

My knight in shining armor.

Thankfully, Liam and Mimi start talking about ranch stuff, and I'm off the hook as the topic of conversation.

I eat until I can't eat another bite. For the first time in a long time, I think I can officially say that I'm full.

"Well, I think I'm going to go draw a bath. Can you two kids handle the cleanup?"

What? She never takes her bath before the kitchen is spotless.

I narrow my eyes toward her.

"Absolutely. Thank you so much for a lovely dinner," Liam says.

I start grabbing dishes and take them to the sink. After Mimi is upstairs, I say, "Why are you such a kiss-ass?"

Liam laughs. "Why are you such an ass?"

I shrug. "Must be the New Yorker in me."

"*Oookaay*," Liam draws out.

"What does that mean?" I ask.

"Nothing," he sighs.

"You know, I don't like you."

He laughs. "I don't like you either, Len."

"Ugh," I groan.

Liam closes the distance between us. His face is hard with anger. I step back until I feel the kitchen sink and pull in a breath. Liam bends down until his face is an inch from mine. He holds on to the counter on either side of my waist, caging me in with his arms. I can smell him, and though I thought it'd be repulsive, it's the complete opposite. Sweat and all, his scent makes my heart beat faster.

"Look at me." His voice sounds strained.

I open my eyes and stare into his.

"I have always been kind to you," Liam whispers. His lips are so close to mine that I can feel his breath. "I don't know why you treat me the way you do, but I don't deserve it. You need to grow the hell up, Leni."

I gasp and press my hands against his chest under the pretense of wanting him to step back from me. Yet, truthfully, I need his lips away from my own because the temptation is too great. Despite what I need, he doesn't budge. If anything, he leans in even closer, and now, I have the added sensation of his hard chest beneath my palms.

He continues, "And, though you're a really good actress, I know you're not any of those things. *I know you.*" He says the last sentence with added emphasis "This isn't you. When you're tired of the games and you decide you want a friend, let me know. I can be a really good friend. But I can't be your punching bag."

He pushes off the counter and away from me. I listen as he walks out, closing the front door behind him. I can't move, frozen in the place he left me.

Holy hell. What just happened?

My body almost shakes with the amount of pent-up desire coursing through it—and for whom? *Liam?* But I don't even like him. *Right?*

I'm so confused.

Listening to my heart—or in this case, body—when it comes to Liam has never been part of the plan, yet now that my plan is shot to hell and I'm back in Texas, living with my grandma, the rules are becoming less black and white. There's a lot of gray, and I'm stuck in it.

I just need to finish the dishes, take a nice hot shower, and get in bed.

I'm tired, so exhausted. I simply need sleep to clear my mind. Tomorrow will be better. I can start on a new plan to get out of here and begin living the life of my dreams. This is just a pit stop, and Liam Moore is just a roadblock. I don't need him as a friend or otherwise.

I don't need anyone.

four

Leni
Age Thirteen

I hate them. I hate them. I hate them.

I glare toward the kitchen where my parents are talking. I don't even attempt to hear what they're saying. It doesn't matter. I haven't uttered a word to them in two weeks. I hope to never speak to them again. I'll never forgive them.

Thinking about it now still makes me sick. I wipe an errant tear that insisted on falling.

I won't cry.

I won't give them the satisfaction of seeing me cry. I'll never let them know how deeply they've shattered my heart. They can't think they've won because they haven't. I'll never stop fighting until I'm out of here. I'm going to go to some fancy art school, and I'm going to be the best artist the world has ever seen.

I'll show them.

Thank God I get to go to Mimi's tomorrow. I suppose they could still take away my time at my grandma's if they wanted. I had to threaten them a couple of weeks ago not to, and though the threat worked and they backed down, they could realize it was all just a threat. I never did take pictures of my bruises that have all but faded now. If they call me on my bluff and take away my summer with Mimi, I might legitimately die of a broken heart.

"Come eat, Eleanora," my mother calls from the dining room.

I begrudgingly walk to the dining room and take my seat. I pick at my dinner while my parents continue to talk.

My ears perk up when my mom starts talking about dance. We don't talk much about her dancing days, but before she and my dad got together, she was a world-class ballerina. She gave up her dreams at his command.

You'd never have known that she'd worked her entire life to perfect her craft. I've seen the pictures. They're all hidden away in a box in the guest bedroom closet, but I found them. There were years of pictures, newspaper articles, and *Nutcracker* programs. I also found my mother's acceptance letter to Juilliard. Apparently, she only completed one year before she met my father. He was a few years older than her and already on his way to establishing his political career. They met at a gala to raise money for the arts. Ironic, seeing that he demanded she leave Juilliard and marry him.

Also ironic is the fact that he had my entire art studio thrown out just two weeks ago because I refused to skip Mimi's this year to go to a snobby equestrian camp. I don't even ride horses. One of his colleague's daughters is going, and he wants an in with the family. I don't care whom my father associates with, but he's not going to take me away from Mimi to accomplish it.

My mother continues, her voice cheerful, "So, Carol asked if I'd be interested in teaching one of the beginning classes. It would only be twice a week. I think it'd be nice to be back in the dance world for a bit."

"No," my father says plainly. "You're not a child anymore, Nora. I've got too much going on right now that you should be helping with. I don't have time for you to hop around a room in a tutu like an idiot twice a week."

My mother grins toward my dad. "No, you're absolutely right. We're much too busy. I'll tell Carol no."

I break my two-week-silence strike. "No! Mom, no! You should do this. It would be so fun."

I shouldn't care about my mom's happiness because she makes it clear daily that she doesn't care about mine. Yet I couldn't keep quiet. My dad's wrong.

"Eleanora!" my dad barks. "Enough."

"No, Dad. This isn't right. Mom used to love to dance. Two nights a week is nothing. It would make her happy," I plead.

"No one asked for your opinion. When you're an adult, you'll understand. Being a grown-up means making grown-up decisions," he sternly tells me.

"He's right. It was a silly idea. I shouldn't have brought it up," Mom says.

God, she's a doormat.

I just shake my head. I want to fight for my mom, but there's no use when she won't even stick up for herself. The conversation between my parents shifts to focus back on my father.

After a bit, my mom places her hand over my father's. "Would you like dessert, sweetie?"

He nods.

She gets up from the table, and before she clears my father's plate, she kisses him on the top of the head. She's always so nice to him, showing affection or telling him that she loves him. I don't know how she could. He's evil.

I think, a long time ago, before I was born, my mom was cool. I mean, she was a dancer. But then she fell in love, and now, she's this person who makes me sick.

I'm never falling in love—like, ever. All love does is change you and hurt you. I'll never be like my mom. I'll never stop loving myself so that I can love another. Never.

I run up to Mimi and throw my arms around her. I've never been so happy to see her in my life. I barely made it through the past nine months without her. I couldn't have made it much longer.

My mother is backing out of the drive before I even get my luggage inside. I watch her Lexus pull away and can't help but feel sad. I wish she were *more*—like a better mom to start with. My sadness is short-lived as Mimi wraps her arm around me, and we take my last bag inside. Yeah, so I have crappy parents, but I'd never trade my Mimi for good ones.

There's a spread of goodness across the table that would rival any Thanksgiving feast. Mimi has made all my favorites.

"Oh my gosh! This all looks amazing. I've missed your cooking." I tightly hug her.

"I can tell, my dear. You're too skinny," Mimi kids.

"You would be, too, if you had to eat Mom's healthy, bland crap."

We sit down at the table.

"Oh, I'm sure it's not that bad." Mimi throws my mother some kindness that she doesn't deserve.

I lower my gaze and stare at her until she starts laughing.

"Okay, I'm sure it's bad." She laughs, and I giggle along with her. "So, tell me everything! What was seventh grade like? I want all the juicy details."

We talk for hours at the kitchen table. I tell her all about my boring private school and my horrible parents. Her smile fades when I tell her some of the things, like how my parents threw out all my art supplies. I don't tell her about how my father kicked me into his desk a few weeks ago, causing me the worst pain I'd ever felt in my life. I know, if I told her, she'd fight to get me taken away from him, and she'd lose. She'd spend all of the money she had for lawyers, and it'd all be for nothing because my father isn't an easy person to beat.

I do tell her most things however. I don't like hurting Mimi, and I know she feels helpless when I'm at home, but at the same time, I really need to talk to someone about everything. My relationship with Mimi is the sole reason that I'm somewhat sane.

Mimi is serving some peach cobbler in the kitchen. "You know, I was thinking that I need to redecorate the living room. Do you think you could help me? I was hoping we could go into town to get some canvases and paint, so you could create some artwork for the new space."

"Yes! I would love that! I can do a really good job."

She sets the bowl of cobbler and vanilla ice cream down in front of me and pats my hand. "Oh, I know you will. You are incredible, Leni girl. Don't you forget it."

After I've eaten all that I can eat, I ask Mimi if I can go see Liam. Besides Mimi, he's the only other person who truly gets me.

Mimi tells me to go, and so I do. Sprinting across Mimi's land toward Liam's with a full belly gives me a huge cramp, but I don't mind because nothing could spoil today. I see him out in the pasture, working on a fence.

His eyes gleam, and his lips turn up into a huge grin when he sees me. He's just turned toward me when I jump into his arms. He spins me around, and I laugh. After he puts me down, I really take him in. I can't believe how different he looks. He's going to be fourteen next week, but he looks like ... I don't know ... a college kid or something. His chest is wider, and his arm muscles seem bigger. His face looks older, like he lost some of his cheeks or something. It's weird, and it makes my belly feel uneasy.

"Are you okay?" He chuckles. "You're staring at me with your mouth open."

I blink hard. "Sorry. I was just thinking about how different you look since last year."

"Oh, yeah? You look different, too."

"Good different?" I ask.

"Oh, definitely."

He shoots me a cute smirk, and it does something to me. I can feel my heart beating hard within my chest. It's like I'm nervous, but I'm never nervous around Liam.

"I'm all done here. Do you want to go swimming in the river?" he asks.

Liam and I spend a lot of our free time in the summers playing in the Llano River. It's such a hot day, and swimming sounds amazing.

"Yes! Let me run home and get my bathing suit."

"Okay. I'll swing by in a minute, and we'll go." He picks up his box of tools and heads toward the barn.

I run back across the field to Mimi's and rifle through my suitcase for my new swimsuit. My mom said she picked me up one at the mall this week and packed it. My jaw drops when I pull it out of the suitcase.

It's official. My mom hates me.

I put on the bikini before looking at myself in the full-length mirror in my bedroom.

Seriously?

The top is two triangles that cover my boobs, tied together with elastic string.

Why would she do this to me?

This is my first summer with real boobs, like I-need-a-supportive-bra boobs. Gone are the trainer-bra boobs of last summer.

I miss my trainer-bra boobs.

I let out a frustrated sigh. I want to cry.

Did she do this to embarrass me?

I shake my head. Even my mom isn't that cruel. She seemed genuinely excited when she told me she got me a new swimsuit. She said that I'd love the pattern and style. It's no surprise that my mother doesn't know me at all.

I hear a man downstairs, talking to Mimi. I open my bedroom door a crack to listen and realize that it's Liam. God, even his voice has changed. I throw on a baggy T-shirt over my suit and slip on my flip-flops before making my way downstairs.

"You kids have fun. Wear your sunscreen, Leni," Mimi reminds me.

"I will," I say before giving her a hug.

Once we're at the river, I take a deep breath and remove my T-shirt.

He's your friend. He's not going to care that you have major boobs now. Just like you don't care that he's all muscly.

I can feel Liam's stare on me, but I pretend that I don't. I squirt the sunscreen lotion onto my arms and rub it in.

"Want me to get your back?" Liam asks.

My head pops up. He is standing before me in his swim trunks. His chest is tan, and his muscles are defined. His deep brown eyes capture mine, and I can't deny the feelings they stir within me.

Liam has applied sunscreen to my back and shoulders every time we've come to the river since I was young. His question isn't an odd one, yet it leaves me feeling really uneasy.

"Yeah, sure," I say.

I pull my hair to the side as Liam rubs his lotioned hands over my skin. I know he's done this countless times, but it feels like this is the first. Every swipe of his palms makes my heart beat faster.

"All done," he says cheerfully.

I turn to face him, and I can't deny the fact that I want him to kiss me.

What? Where did that come from?

I've never kissed anyone in my life, and I certainly don't want to kiss Liam.

"Are you okay?" He places his hand on my shoulder. "You seem different. What'd your parents do this time?"

I look into his eyes, so kind, and now, I'm admitting for the first time that they're so beautiful. My bottom lip begins to quiver as realization dawns. I like Liam. I *like* him.

My eyes fill with tears, and Liam pulls me into a hug. "Len, what is it?"

I allow Liam to hold me in his arms as I cry. My heart breaks as I sob in my stupid bikini with my stupid boobs and Liam's stupid deep voice and handsome face.

Life is so unfair. I've never felt like this before, but I know that this must be what falling in love feels like. I suppose I'm not surprised.

What did I expect?

My best friend is kind, funny, and gorgeous. Mix in the fact that he's also a guy, and it's a recipe for disaster. Dumb hormones. I totally realize that this is what my health teacher was talking about when she went on and on about hormones and changes and feelings.

I don't want anything to change.

But everything's changed.

Everything is ruined.

I can't be Liam's friend anymore. I can't risk falling in love. I will never be my mother. I will never fall in love.

I look at Liam. "I'm an artist," I sob. "I'm leaving Texas, and I'm never coming back."

Liam stares at me, his eyes wide. He's clearly at a loss for words.

"I'm not staying here. As soon as I can leave, I'm gone. I'm not going to change myself for anyone." I cry, years of memories of my parents' *love* invading my mind, and I shudder.

"Okay," Liam says calmly. "It's okay, Len. Whatever it is, it's okay." He rubs my back.

"It's not." I shake my head and step back from him. "I can't be your friend anymore."

"What?" Liam's expression is one of complete confusion.

"Just leave me alone, William. Don't ever talk to me again!" I say through tears before I turn and run as fast as I can, away from the river, away from Liam, and away from my fears.

I hear him calling my name from behind me, but I don't stop. I'll never stop. I have too much to lose.

five

Liam

My arm is spread across the back of the couch. Camila leans back against the crook of my arm, her long, thin fingers tracing circles atop my jean clad thigh. I'm engulfed in the familiar smells, ones I've grown accustomed to over the past few months but never craved—those of designer perfumes, hair products, and lotions. Particularly offensive today is the man-made odor rising from the chunk of plastic plugged into the electric outlet beside me. It's an ill attempt at flowers, I think. Maybe lavender?

It's assaulting to my senses and the complete opposite of what I long for.

Some of my favorite scents are of dirt, wet with morning dew; fresh-cut hay, earthy and clean; or the mild sweetness of a young cornstalk when its leaves are still bright green and new. I'm met with these nostalgic scents on a daily basis in my line of work, and it fills me with peace, knowing that I'm doing exactly what I was always meant to.

There's a suppressed part of my soul that knows all of my favorite things are intertwined with recollections of *her*.

Good memories. Tragic ones, too.

I attempt to separate the two, not willing to lose the good. Every once in a while, they creep up regardless, more so lately now that she's back and my heart is forced to feel her presence. She was so ingrained in everything. Three months a year, we were each other's shadow, only separated when life dictated it so. The other nine months of the year, she was my best friend from afar. Many moments not dedicated to school or chores were spent corresponding with Leni through instant message or e-mail.

She was my constant.

Until she wasn't.

A chance meeting with a bubbly, green-eyed girl in a cornfield changed my life, and I'm still reeling from its effect.

Bending down, I take a stick and draw an arrow in the earth beneath my feet. The leaves of the cornstalks on either side of me brush against my arms. The sun is straight above me, shining down brightly. It's hot, but then it's always hot here.

There's a crunch behind me, the sound of a long leaf from a stalk breaking. I slowly turn around, hoping to see a deer up close. I take a step back, startled, when I see her. She's not scary, just unexpected.

"Why are you drawing arrows?" she asks with a smile, her bright green eyes shining with curiosity.

I tilt my head to the side and take her in. She's probably about my age, maybe a little younger, with long brown braids hanging down on either side of her shoulders. She has a spattering of freckles across her nose and a smile that makes me move closer toward her.

"How old are you?" I ask.

"Six."

"I'm six, too. But I'll be seven in a couple of weeks. What's your name?"

"Leni," she answers, and for some reason, her name makes me happy.

"I'm Liam. Where do you live?"

She shakes her head. "I don't live here. But I'm staying with Mimi for the summer." She points toward the Turner farm.

"Oh. So, Mrs. Turner is your grandma?"

She nods, causing her braids to bounce against her skin.

"I live over there." I raise my arm, my finger extending in the direction of my dad's farm.

"What's the arrow for?" she asks again.

"I'm marking a path through the corn to my secret hideout, so I don't forget how to get there."

"You have a secret hideout?" Her eyebrows rise along with her voice.

"Not yet. But I will. I'm looking for the perfect spot now."

"I can help you. I'm really good at finding things."

I think about her offer, and the more I think about it, the more excited I become. The only person who lives close to us at all is Mrs. Turner. I never have anyone to play with. I only just met Leni, but I already like her.

"Okay. I think that will be fun. We can make a hideout just for us."

Leni jumps up onto her tiptoes and claps, a wide smile spreading across her face, and I can't help but smile back.

"Hey, did you hear me?"

I blink and look to Camila.

"I'm sorry. What?" No, I didn't hear her. I haven't been able to stop the Leni-filled memories from flooding my mind since I almost hit her a few days ago.

"You're distracted tonight, huh? Has the ranch been crazy busy?" She leans into me and places her hand on my chest. Her candy-red lips are mere inches from mine as she whispers, "I know something we can do to relieve your stress."

Camila's beautiful, no doubt. I study her features, maybe truly for the first time. As a package, she's cover-model material. Yet, when I really start to look, I realize that I don't know what she really looks like. Her eyelashes are fake, always long and dark. I've never seen her without makeup. I don't know what type she uses, but her bright red lips will still look the same after hours of activity in her bed. She gets her nails done every other week at the salon. She never has a hair out of place. Her boobs are fake, not that I've ever had any complaints about them. I'd be lying if I said she wasn't good in bed because she is. She's amazing in bed.

Camila kisses my neck and splays her hands across my chest. I know she'd feel so good right now, if I could just turn off my mind.

I can't get Leni out of my head. Every time I close my eyes, I see her. The moment I first saw her startled greens staring at me as she stood inches in front of my truck, the sensation of the air leaving my lungs, feels like it happened just moments ago. It's fresh in my mind, and my body still craves that woman. She wasn't wearing an ounce of makeup, and yet she was—and is—the most beautiful woman I'd ever seen.

And I've always seen her.

Through every stage in Leni's life, regardless of how many layers of protection that she's piled on, she's always been transparent to me. I've seen the way she loves, her fears, her sadness, and the way she hides.

I've seen her eyes, as green as the newest grass, full of life as it grows toward the sun. I've seen her hair, rich chocolate and the way it shines with hints of red in the sunlight. I've seen her smile, her stunning smile, which could brighten up the darkest room. I have every detail of her body memorized—well, the parts I've seen anyway. I can close my eyes and imagine it all—her soft skin, her curves, the small freckles on her nose, her voice, her smell.

I can see now that she's scared and sad, though I'm not completely sure why or of what. But I want to know. I want to be the person to help her face her fears and find her joy. The idea that I should be the one to help her with these things is absurd. I've been so far removed from Leni and her life up north for so long. She made it clear years ago that she didn't want me to be in her life.

Yet I can see through that lie, too. She needs me. She believes she doesn't, but I know different.

I gave my heart to Eleanora Turner years ago without even realizing I had, and I've never gotten it back. And, despite everything—the way in which she's treated me and her harsh words—I don't want it back. I know that my Leni is still there, hiding behind those piercing greens. I think she's waiting for me to find her.

Camila's lips tug on my earlobe as her hand moves down my pants. I wrap my hand around her wrist, halting her descent.

"Wait." I scoot away from her, turning so that I can look her in the eyes. "I can't."

"You can't?" She tilts her head to the side, pursing her lips. "You're not in the mood?"

"No, that's not it. Well, kind of." I stumble on my words. "I mean, you're right; I'm not in the mood, but there's more. I can't do this anymore." I move my hand back and forth between us. "Us ... whatever we are. I can't do it."

Camila and I have never had a label. We hang out a couple of times a week, and for the most part, we have sex. Yet I hesitate to say we're in a real relationship because the depth isn't there. She doesn't spend time with my family, nor do I with hers. We don't talk about the future or basically anything that matters.

"You want to break up?" Her eyes go wide.

Can two people break up if they've never officially gotten together?

"I want to end things, yes."

"Why?" she snaps.

"I just have a lot on my mind. It's not fair to you. And, truthfully, I don't really see us going anywhere."

She throws her head back and laughs, which throws me off guard. "You're such a girl, Liam. I don't see this 'going anywhere'"—she bends her fingers in air quotes— "either, but who cares? We can still have fun. We're really good at the having-fun part." The corner of her lip tilts up, and she moves in closer, splaying her hand across my thigh.

I place my hand on hers, stopping its movement upward, and stand. "I'm sorry. I have to go."

She rolls her eyes. "Okay. Whatever."

"I'll catch ya around," I say.

"Whatever," she repeats.

I get into my truck. As I pull away from Camila's, I feel unsettled. Now that Leni's back at the farm, I can't turn my mind off. I know I need to do something. I'm just not sure what. For now, I'm simply going to go on with my days as I normally would, and hopefully, the rest will fall into place.

I don't know why Leni's back.

I have no idea what she needs, but I'm hoping to help her find it.

So much has changed since the last time I saw Leni, but the things that matter haven't changed a bit. Underneath all the hurt, she's still the same girl, and I'm still the same boy who fell in love with my best friend. True, I didn't know I was falling at the time. Maybe I've been falling since, and maybe it's finally time to stop.

Six

Leni

My back presses against the same floral upholstered sofa that's been in this exact spot in the living room my entire life. My head against the armrest, I stare at the old ceiling. The same fine cracks in the plaster are right where I remember them, spreading out like a spiderweb.

I'm not sure if Mimi even realizes these faint lines exist. Yet I know them well. Liam and I used to lie on the floor and stare at the ceiling, pretending the barely visible cracks were in fact a secret treasure map. We'd discuss where the paths must lead and how to get to the treasure. We'd plan and then go outside and search for our riches.

A new line has splintered off from the most prominent one, creating an unimposing cluster of its own in the far corner of the room. In all my time of studying this map as a child, not once did a new path form. Now, I lie here, completely taken aback by the fact that new cracks have formed since I left. Sometimes, I can pretend that it's been a matter of months since I've been back here. Everything's the same. This place is like a time capsule that never changes, and there's something comforting about that.

Yet, when I see Mimi and the way her face has wrinkled with age and now this ceiling and the new addition to my childhood adventure map, it reminds me that it's been five very long years. Five years of searching for myself and finding nothing. Years of distancing myself from this state and everything it stands to take away from me. It was wasted time.

I'm no closer to finding myself than I was when I left for New York, right out of high school. I've spent the last five years filling my soul with everything I thought it needed to become whole, and yet I lie here, empty, nonetheless.

"Leni love, Emily's on her way over here to get you. Do you want to get changed?" Mimi's words break into my self-loathing pity party.

"What?" I ask her, as I'm sure I didn't hear her correctly.

"Emily's on her way to pick you up. You ready?"

Crap. I guess I did hear her correctly.

"Seriously?" I ask as I sit up so fast that my head feels dizzy. "Emily Jacobs? As in the girl I haven't seen or spoken to in years?"

Mimi nods and smiles sweetly as if she didn't just overstep her bounds and role as my grandmother. I'm past the point in life where I need a playdate organized on my behalf.

I pull in air through my nose in an attempt to calm down, so I don't yell at Mimi, which I have never done in my entire life but am dangerously close to doing at this moment.

"No," I say simply, shaking my head. "I'm not going."

"She's about ten minutes out if you want to change," Mimi states, ignoring my previous declaration as she wipes the kitchen table.

"I don't want to hang out with Emily. I haven't seen her in years. We have nothing in common. It will be completely awkward."

"Well, I saw her grandmother, Mavis, at church, and she was telling me how excited Emily was to hear that you're back in town. So, we set something up. It will be great. You need to get out of the house. It will be good for you to hang out with your old friends."

I scoff, "We're not even friends, Mimi."

I spent a little time with Emily during the summers of my teenage years after I pushed Liam away but only because Mimi was so worried about me and the fact that I wasn't hanging out with Liam anymore. My friendship with Emily was nothing more than a weak attempt to placate Mimi, so she wouldn't reach out to Liam to facilitate *patching things up* between the two of us.

I haven't thought about Emily Jacobs since I left Texas.

Mimi waves her hand through the air, dismissing my statement as if being friends has anything to do with it. "Just give it a minute, and you two will be two peas in a pod, just like you used to be."

"We were never even that close." I peer toward Mimi as if she'd grown two heads, clueless ones at that.

"So, you're wearing your pajamas out then?" Mimi scans my attire.

I look down toward the boxer shorts and baggy T-shirt that I've been living in for the past couple of days. "You know this little playdate that you organized is going to seriously cut into my sulking time."

"That's the plan," she quips brightly.

A minute later, I'm coming down the stairs in an outfit other than my pajamas to the sounds of Mimi and Emily chatting in the front room.

"Leni!" Emily shrieks when she sees me and pulls me into a hug.

"Hey, Em," I say back with as much excitement as I can muster.

I frown pleadingly at Mimi as I follow Emily toward the door. Mimi returns my frown with a reassuring grin, though it does little to make me feel better.

When we're outside, I take a moment to really look at Emily. She looks almost the same as she did in high school. She's wearing her long blonde hair in a ponytail. Her face is makeup-free and as adorable as it's always been. Her button nose is spattered with light freckles, and the dimple in her cheek is still present when she smiles, which she does all of the time. She's a happy, bubbly little princess of small-town Texas.

Then, I notice the belly, her round and out-of-place belly.

"Are you pregnant?" I blurt out.

Emily giggles, and a huge smile crosses her face. "Yeah, six months."

"Oh my gosh," I say, bewildered. I can't imagine being pregnant right now, let alone being happy about it.

"Whose baby is it?"

"My husband's." She grins.

"You're married? To whom?"

She stops and looks at me with a squint to her eye. "Westley," she says with a tilt of her head as if she can't believe I didn't know.

I didn't know. I had no idea that Emily would marry her boyfriend from high school.

I know Westley, though I avoided him as much as I could during my summers here because he was friends with Liam. From what I remember, he was a nice enough guy, but as I look at little knocked-up, married Emily, I'm sad for her.

"It's a good thing, Len."

My facial expression must not be hiding as much of my thoughts as I would've hoped.

We get into Emily's car, and she pulls onto the road.

Emily chats idly, catching me up on everything Elkwood, as she drives us to Twisters, the little family-owned ice cream place in town. I'm feeling a sense of déjà vu as I listen. Same people, same stories, different day. I hate that my ears perk up when she mentions Liam, but they do.

"Have you seen him yet?" she asks.

"Just once, briefly, when I first got into town," I tell her.

"Well, he's dating Camila."

"Camila Banks?" I ask, though I already know the answer.

There's only one Camila in this town, and everyone knows her. She's the daughter of Edgar Banks, who owns the grocery store in Elkwood along with several others in neighboring towns. For a place like this, a man who owns a handful of stores is a pretty big deal, and Camila grew up thinking she was a local celebrity. Her years in the pageant circle didn't help shrink her bloated ego either. She's exactly what my parents always wished I'd be. I never liked her, and I can't lie and say that the fact that Liam is dating her doesn't bother me.

"The one and only." Emily chuckles.

"What does he see in her?"

"I'm not sure."

Emily parks, and we each order a fudge-dipped ice cream cone. It's the worst kind of cone to order in Texas because the chocolate shell starts melting almost immediately in the heat. I have to scramble to eat the chocolate before it melts down my hand, but Emily and I always order it.

We sit on the table beneath the red-and-white-striped umbrella. "Does Westley still hang out with Liam?" I ask between licks.

"Yeah, sometimes. They're both so busy with work, but when they can, they hang out."

Admittedly, it's pretty easy to talk with Emily. My reservations on hanging out with her initially had more to do with me and my own self-pity than it did with Emily. I know that. Mimi, once again, was right. Getting outside and interacting with another person is helping my mood. For goodness' sake, my entire plan for the day, prior to this, consisted of staring at the ceiling.

"Do you want to see our house?" Emily asks, referring to her and Westley's home.

"Sure."

Emily and Westley live in a small brick ranch downtown. It's a cute little starter home. Emily beams with pride as she tells me all about it—from how they decided that this was the right house, to why they chose different color schemes for each room, to their decision on whether or not to use the small space off of the kitchen as a formal dining area or a sitting area.

She leads me to one of the bedrooms, which is completely empty, save for a mint-green upholstered rocking chair. "This is going to be the baby's room."

"Do you know what you're having?"

"No, not yet." She reaches for a sealed envelope that rests on a shelf on the sidewall. "Though the answer's in here." She grins wide. "We're going back and forth on whether we should find out or be surprised. I want it to be a surprise, but honestly, I think we might crack and open the envelope. It's really hard to decorate a nursery when you don't know what you're having."

"Well, green could be for either." I motion toward the one piece of furniture in the room.

"I know, which is why we originally got it. But, now, I find myself wanting to get purple items to go with the mint green. Don't you think that would look great?"

"Yeah, it would be pretty."

"Exactly, but not for a boy."

"Boys can like purple." I shrug.

"True, but we'd probably do more of a green-and-blue sports theme for a little boy. Westley has been waiting his whole life for a son. If it's a boy, you'd better believe he'll go all out with the sports stuff."

"Girls like sports, too."

Emily nods. "I know that, if it's a girl, she's going to be crazy into sports like her daddy. So, most likely, my only chance to give her a princess room is when she's little before her daddy corrupts her into the world of football and baseball."

"Not a sports fan?" I ask.

"Not at all." Emily chuckles.

"Me either," I agree.

"I think we might end up doing one of those gender-reveal parties with the pink or blue balloons coming out of a box or breaking something to be showered with pink or blue confetti. I'm not sure yet."

It's hard to believe that I'm in a conversation about how to celebrate whether one is pregnant with a boy or a girl, and I'm actually enjoying the dialogue. It's weird and not me. This entire day with Emily has been out of my comfort zone, but I have been having a great time. There's something about Emily that makes me feel at ease. Truthfully, she's simply a nice person. She legitimately cares for others and wants the best for them. She doesn't have ulterior motives when talking to me. It's refreshing.

"Want some iced tea?" Emily asks.

"Sure." I nod.

She hands me a glass of tea, and we take a seat on the sofa in the living room.

"I feel like I've done all the talking today. I can't help myself. I'm a chatterbox." She chuckles. "Tell me about you. How've you been? How was art school? New York? Do you have a boyfriend?" she rambles off questions in rapid succession.

The biggest saving grace about today was the fact that I could rely on Emily to fill any awkward silences with lighthearted conversation, and I didn't feel like I had to talk. It was nice, getting out of my head for a while because, truthfully, my thoughts as of late have been quite depressing.

"Not much. School was fine. New York was fine. No boyfriend. That's about all."

"How long are you staying with your grandma?"

"Until I can find a job that will support me. An art degree doesn't always translate to a good job, unfortunately."

"Yeah, that would be hard." She frowns, and on her face, I see actual concern for me.

"I'll find something and get out of this state as soon as I can."

She laughs. "What's so bad about Texas?"

"I just can't be here."

"But why?"

"You want the truth?" I ask.

"Of course."

I know the words that are about to come out of my mouth have the potential to sound rude and condescending, but these thoughts have been suffocating me since I left my apartment in New York. I need to get them out.

"I don't want to be trapped. I don't want to be tied down, married, pregnant, and stuck somewhere. Maybe it's fine for you, and if that's the case, then great. But it's not okay for me. It would kill me. Do you ever feel like you're stuck here?"

"No, Leni," Emily scoffs. Her hand goes to her belly, and she absentmindedly rubs it. "I'm happy. I'm not trapped in this life. This is the life I chose. This"—she circles her arm around—"is everything I've ever wanted."

"But this will be your life forever."

"I know. How great is that?" She smiles wide, and it throws me off guard. "You know I love you, Leni. But, if we're being honest here ... you've always been a little too judgmental. You have to realize that what might be your dream or best for you isn't what's best for others. All I've ever wanted is to be a good person, wife, and mother. That's more than enough for me. There's nothing about my dreams that makes them less important than yours. Being a wife and a mother is my ultimate dream."

"I know. You're right," I tell Emily, and I mean it.

She's nothing like my mother, and I feel guilty, lumping her into the same category with the woman who raised me.

She tilts her head. "But do you really know? Do you get it, or are you just saying that so as not to hurt my feelings?" She gently moves her glass around, causing the ice cubes to swirl in the tea. "I remember so many of our conversations when we were younger revolved around your desire to get as far away from here as possible. You never went into details, but I knew that you weren't happy. I wanted all of your dreams to come true for you because everyone deserves happiness."

She presses her lips together in a grin, and I bite mine, warding off the unwanted emotions that this conversation is bringing.

"You did everything you said you'd do. You left Texas. You went to a great art school and got a degree. Yet you're back, and excuse me if I'm overstepping, but you still don't seem happy. You seem like the same teenage girl who was filled with so much anger and angst. Everyone deserves to find their purpose, Leni, their happiness. I just don't think your path is leading you there. If anything, the past few years have just led you back here."

"I know. That's the problem." I let out a sigh.

"Is this place and the people here really the problem?" She shakes her head. "I don't think it is. Who knows? Maybe you'll find that what you need has been here all along."

"Doubtful." I scrunch up my face.

Emily stands and takes our glasses to the kitchen. "All I'm saying is that you've heard people talk about the definition of insanity. Right?"

"Yeah, doing the same thing over and over and expecting different results."

"Exactly." She comes back into the living room. "For as long as I've known you, you've blamed your unhappiness on this place and these people. You're still unhappy, and you're still blaming this place and these people. Change it up, Len. Find another route toward your purpose. Your current one isn't working." She shoots me a wink.

I roll my eyes and attempt a scowl, but I can't muster one. A grin finds my lips. As much as I want to be annoyed with Emily, the girl has some fair points. I'm not sure how I'll change or what I'll do. She's right though. I've been sad for a long time. I've been angry even longer. I'm desperate to find joy. I've worked so hard to reach it, and yet it always eludes me. I'm tired of failing. I could really use a win, and though I know that change is needed, I have no clue where to start.

Seven

Leni
Age Sixteen

"I don't want to go," I stand tall as I address Mimi, who's perched on the end of my bed, a *Better Homes and Gardens* magazine spread across her lap.

"I think it will be good for you. You can't just hang out with an old lady all the time." She flips the page with a snap.

"I like hanging out with you, and you're not old. You're actually pretty young for a grandma." I cautiously eye her, hoping the compliment—which is a hundred percent true—helps my case.

"You're going," she continues smoothly. "You need friends your own age."

I peer into the mirror above my dresser and pick at the purple hair atop my head, separating the random spiky chunks out more evenly. I clear my throat. "You know there might be alcohol there."

Her eyes stay trained on the article before her. "Then, don't drink it."

"Everyone's going to stare at my purple hair," I tell her, feeling strangely self-conscious.

Mimi looks up from her reading material. "If you don't want to draw attention to yourself, then don't dye your hair purple."

"I like it purple, and I don't care what anyone else thinks."

The side of her lip turns up into a grin. "Then, I see no problem."

I hold my black lipstick in my hand, an essential staple of my daily look back home, contemplating. I drop it into my makeup bag and grab the clear lip gloss.

"You know my entire look is to piss off my mom," I tell Mimi as I swipe some gloss over my lips.

"Oh, I know that," she responds with a small chuckle.

"In fact, I think I'm going to dye my hair green before heading home in August. She'll just love that." I pop my lips together, rubbing in the gloss.

"I'm sure she will." Mimi shakes her head. "You about ready?"

I run my hand over my black leather wristbands with silver spikes lying across the top of the dresser and opt to go without my routine accessories tonight. This is small-town Texas; my purple hair and horrible attitude push the limits enough as it is. Plus, my mom isn't here to see me, so the extra time needed to apply all of my dark makeup and leather bands would be a waste.

"Yeah, I'm ready," I say to my reflection, which, besides my disheveled amethyst locks, appears quite normal.

Boring.

I'm sure all the other girls at the party will be wearing jean shorts and a tight shirt of some sort as well. At least my little T-shirt is black; it has that going for it.

It doesn't matter. I'm only going to appease Mimi. I realized last summer that, the more I hang out with Emily, the less Mimi asks about Liam, and I seriously need her to stop asking me about Liam. I don't want to think about him because, when I do, it hurts—a lot. I miss him.

Honestly, I don't mind Emily. She's pretty cool. I'm leery of tonight though because it's a barn party, and Emily is dating Westley, one of Liam's friends. I'm sure Liam will stop by. It's awkward between us now, to say the least. Cutting one's best friend out of one's life is messy and complicated and painful, and no amount of purple hair dye will shield me from the consequences of it.

Emily holds my hand as she pulls me toward the big barn. The grass is tall and scratches at my legs as we walk.

"I really can't believe it's been a whole school year already. Did your sophomore year just fly by, too? I'm sure Westley had something to do with it. I'm not going to lie; I'm mildly obsessed with him. He's just so sweet. I really want you to get to know him more this summer. He's going to be a senior this year, like Liam. I'm going to miss him so much when he goes off to college next year. I mean, I know that's still over a year away, but it's something to think about. God, I haven't shut up since you got in my car. I've hardly let you get two words in. Just tell me to shut up," Emily says with a giggle.

"Shut up," I say in all seriousness before cracking a smile. "Kidding." I nudge her arm with mine. "Talk all you want. It just means I don't have to."

"You're an odd duck, Leni Turner." Emily chuckles. "Okay, I'll let you off the hook tonight, but we will be having some serious chats this summer about your life. I know, over the past nine months, you've done something worth sharing." She pauses. "Well, besides exploring new hairdos, which, by the way, looks adorable on you. You look like a little fairy, a purple Tinker Bell."

I whip around my face, utterly baffled. "I don't want to be Tinker Bell."

Emily stares back with an amused expression. "Well, anyway … you look cute. I bet you'll end up hooking up with someone tonight." She shoots me a wink.

"I don't date."

"Right, right. I know; you don't date," she repeats my words, a hint of exasperation lining her voice. "Doesn't mean you can't hook up."

"I don't do that either," I tell her. "At least, not until college." *When I'm out of Texas and there's no chance of me being stuck here.* I know that hook-ups lead to feelings, which lead to poor decisions. I don't go into all of this now, but Emily's heard my reasoning before.

"Fine, but at least talk to people. Otherwise, you'll be sitting around, watching Westley and me make out." She giggles again.

"Can't wait."

The barn party is exactly what I thought it'd be— people my age, beer, a bonfire, bales of straw as seating, country music blaring, and randomly scattered make-out sessions throughout.

"So, when did you get back in town, Leni?" Westley asks before taking a sip of his beer, his free hand entwined with Emily's.

She is looking up to him with stars in her eyes, as if he hung the moon, and I guess, for her, he did.

They've been attached at the hip since we got here. Emily wasn't joking when she said she was obsessed.

"A couple of weeks ago," I offer.

He nods politely. "Do you have any plans to ..." His question breaks off, and I startle as he yells over me, his smile going wide, "Look who finally showed up! If it isn't the birthday boy himself."

I don't have to turn around to know who just walked in. I remembered the second I woke today that it was Liam's seventeenth birthday. But I turn to look anyway.

My heart plunges in my chest to a place so dark that it's hard to see straight. I swallow hard and plaster on a face of nonchalance. Liam is more beautiful than he was last year. Seventeen looks good on him, though I personally think he looks more like twenty. He looks years older than he did last summer. He's taller, wider, and more muscular—no doubt due to the hours he spends working on the ranch.

His face is still Liam, beautiful in all the ways that make me long for him. He's the boy next door on steroids, and I suppose he literally is that for me—minus the muscle-enhancing drugs. He's lived next to Mimi his whole life, and for a time—which passed far too quickly—he was mine.

Yet how could I keep him when he wasn't mine to have?

I have a plan, and though it makes me ache, Liam's not a part of it. It has to be this way. Every time I want to pretend that it doesn't, I think of my mom and my dad, and it strengthens my resolve. I have to remind myself that a little bit of him would never be enough.

I'd want all of him.

I'd stay for him.

Give up everything for him.

I'd turn into my mom for him.

Liam lifts his chin. "Hey. How are you?" His words speak to indifference, but I hear the slight quiver to his voice.

"Fine. You?" I press my lips into a line, my endeavor to smile falling short.

Westley clears his throat. "Yeah, I'm going to grab another beer. You want one, Liam?"

"Sure. Thanks, man," Liam answers.

Emily and Westley retreat toward the other end of the barn, leaving Liam and me alone in an awkward silence.

He lowers his gaze and kicks the toe of his brown Ariat cowboy boot into the dusty earth, the cadence of the worn leather hitting the ground shrouding the rampant beats of my heart.

He swallows and brings his hesitant stare to mine. There's so much there—worry and want mixed with an underlying familiarity. His gaze reflects my own. Part of me wants to throw my arms around him in an embrace because he's *my Liam.* But then I have to remind myself that he's not—at least, not anymore. He can't be.

"How's your summer been?" he asks, keeping the tone of the conversation safe.

"Fine." I shrug.

"Mimi's good?"

"Yeah."

He eyes my hair. "It looks good on you."

I shake my head. "No, it doesn't. It's ridiculous."

A smile finds Liam's lips, and the ache in my chest intensifies.

"You could pull off pretty much anything. Was your mom pissed?"

"Completely. I'm going to go green next."

He raises an eyebrow. "Green?"

I nod.

He shakes his head. "She's going to love that. Your dad, too."

"My dad pretty much ignores me at this point. The only reactions I get are from my mom."

I should ask Liam about his family or himself, but that would lead him to believe that I care, and though I do, I can't, not when I'm this close to leaving Texas behind.

"So ..." Liam's thoughts fail him.

"So ..." I repeat.

Years of my unpredictable behavior bury us in insecurity. Every summer, I play the game of pushing Liam away when my heart wants to hold him close. He's dealt with unwarranted anger and outbursts from me, evident now in our silence.

What is there to say?

Where do we go when all I've been pushing for is an end? The apparent closure of our strained relationship is so close that I can feel it. I sense it in Liam's stolen glances as he memorizes my features—not sure if or when he'll see them again. There's a hesitancy in our conversation that's in line with awkward strangers meeting for the first time, not lifelong friends.

Liam's chest rises as he pulls in a deep breath. He stands tall, emitting a calm resolution. My skin prickles, and I feel the confrontation coming.

"So, what's the deal for this summer?" he asks, his voice steady. "Are we friends? Are we not? We should probably establish that now, yeah?"

"Nothing's changed on my end." I let out a sigh.

He stares off as he bites on his bottom lip. He returns his attention back to me. "In that we can't hang out because it'll affect your ability to leave? Is that the story you're still going with?"

"It's the only story there is—the truth," I say.

Liam scoffs and drags his fingers through his hair on a long exhale. "You're insane. You know that, right?"

"Whatever." I shrug. "I don't need you to understand."

He shoves his hands in his pockets. "I don't understand because it doesn't make any fucking sense, Len. Like, none. How does our friendship affect anything in the future? Your logic is idiotic."

"Maybe to you it is. Not to me." I shake my head. "You don't have to understand it. You just have to accept it for what it is. Our friendship isn't good for me. That's it. Not all relationships last forever, Liam. It's time to let it go."

Liam pins me with his stare, full of hurt, and it almost breaks me. "I'm not going to try anymore."

"Good. I don't want you to," I force out the words.

If a heart shattering had a sound, it would be one of silence. With these final statements, all of the broken pieces of my heart plummet to the dusty floor where I know they find Liam's destroyed fragments. Yet we don't utter a word.

Fear changes a person. It can rob one of everything if it's great enough. As much as not having Liam in my life kills me, the alternative—loving him—would be worse. I owe it to myself to keep fighting even though I want to surrender, to be strong when I want to be weak, to push him away when all I want to do is hold him close. I deserve happiness. I can't give up when I'm so close to breaking free.

Fear has changed me in ways I've yet to understand. The truth of my reality is that I'm very afraid.

"Well, have a good summer," Liam says, his tone contradictory to his words.

"Yeah, you, too," I whisper.

I watch Liam walk away. On the other side of the barn, he's greeted by drunken cheers. Beer is shoved into his hand. He smiles, seemingly unaffected by our conversation, though I know he is anything but.

He's surrounded by people while I stand alone, but I've always been more comfortable that way.

Camila and Bella approach him. Bella grabs his arm in flirtation, and I can only watch from a distance. Pride tells me to avert my gaze, but desire holds it steady on Liam. I've met these girls before, typical Southern belles who wear the right clothes, look perfect, and carry themselves with an air of superiority. I hate girls like them, though they are exactly who my parents wish I would be.

Bella, with her short shorts and long legs, takes Liam's hand and steals him away from the group. The two of them stand in the opposite corner, their conversation intense. They're locked in a private moment, and I continue to watch like the creeper I am. What does he have in common with her? I am—*was* his best friend, and I'm clearly nothing like her. Though Liam and I haven't been close for a couple of years. He could've changed.

She stands up on her tiptoes, and her hands splay across Liam's chest as she leans toward him. I want to yell at her to stop, but that's not my place. I have no place where Liam is concerned.

Don't, I hope.

But he does.

Her lips press against his. He stills for a fraction of a second and then brings his hands to her hips. I see the moment he gives in to the kiss, his movements becoming more confident, secure. My eyes fill with tears as their kiss intensifies, but I don't let them fall. I won't cry over William Moore. I pushed him away, so I'd never have to shed a tear over him. I should want him to be with someone else.

Unable to look away, I back up until I'm at the large barn door entrance. I step out into the night, ripping myself from the sight of Liam's lips, his hands, his body wanting her. I lean my back against the rough wooden siding of the barn. Pressing my hands to my chest, I breathe in the hot night air. It's of little relief to the agony raging within my chest, but I continue to breathe.

In. Out.

In. Out.

The pain will abate. *It will.* It has to.

This is what I don't want. This is exactly why I close myself off.

Loving Liam would ruin everything, and that's why my only option is to hate him—and I do. I hate him so much.

I hate my mom and my dad and their messed up expectations. I hate everything about Texas, especially the self-centered teenage girls who live here and are everything I'm not. I hate that doing the right thing for my future hurts so much.

My heart is a traitor, but I always knew it had the capability to be one.

I despise the small fragment of my treacherous heart that wants to ignore everything just to have Liam. It makes me weak.

I'm so full of hatred, but I hate being weak the most.

eight

Leni

It's been a couple of weeks since I stood in this kitchen, pushing my hands against Liam's chest. I haven't seen him since, though he's rarely left my mind. It's frustrating, to say the least. I'm trying to change things up, as Emily suggested. Though I've come to realize that change is real damn hard, especially for me. As much as I despise my father, I can't deny that his stubborn streak is thriving within me.

I've decided that my first step to the new me is focusing less on Liam and more on myself and what I need to be happy. So far, I'm failing in that endeavor. I haven't had any interaction with Liam, but that doesn't mean I haven't been obsessed with him nonetheless. I sometimes hear him working in the barn and see him driving his truck out toward the pasture, but I don't dare let him see me. I've pretty much become a twenty-three-year-old recluse. Besides the afternoon I spent with

Emily, I've ventured out to the *city* only once to buy a cell phone charger. Mimi shoved a twenty-dollar bill in my hand and insisted I go get one, so I could catch up with all my friends. I know she's worried about me.

So, after a week of zero contact with my New York friends, I power up my phone, expecting to see hundreds of notifications and text messages. Okay, maybe not hundreds but at least a few. There are none. Literally not one call, text, or tag. I truly thought I'd have plenty of text messages and social media tags and notifications to reply to. There wasn't one photo compilation post of me and my friends on Facebook where they tagged me in a heartfelt message of how much they missed me.

I've never felt lower or more lost in my life. I'm a hamster stuck on a wheel of never-ending failure. I left Texas five years ago—angry, lost, and friendless—and I've returned just the same. The only thing that's changed is, I have a college degree to my name, but I'm coming to find out that a piece of paper entitled as a diploma isn't in fact the key to an amazing future.

I was so determined to make it, to break free of who my parents wanted me to be, that I became jaded and perpetually stuck. I don't know how to find myself.

My phone has been shut off for a few days now since I haven't paid my bill, and I have no desire to turn it back on. What's the point? I'm twenty-three, and I have nothing to show for my life. I have an expensive college degree that I can't use and no true relationships. My entire existence is a facade.

My days are spent watching daytime soap operas, which, truthfully, I had no idea still existed. Mimi doesn't have cable, so there is no HGTV or A&E. There are three numbered channels—four if the aluminum foil antenna is pointing directly toward the eastern corner of the living room. I've also been helping Mimi can everything from peaches to pickles. We have more jars of tomatoes than I could eat in a lifetime.

"All right, Mimi. Last box." I pick up a cardboard box full of glass jars of mushy red tomatoes from the kitchen counter.

"Just put it in the pantry with the rest, Leni love. Thank you. I'm going to run into town for a few things. Would you like to come with me?"

"No, go ahead, Mimi. I have stuff to do here."

She presses her lips together and squints her eyes but decides against arguing about it. "All righty then. Any requests for dinner?"

"You know, whatever you make, I'll love," I answer.

"Okay, I'll be back in a bit." She lays her apron on the counter, grabs her purse, and heads out.

Opening the side kitchen door, I cautiously step out into the small addition that Pops put in for Mimi years ago. I've always found this part of the house so creepy. The floor is a cold concrete, and the walls are made of stone. It's dark and musty—the complete opposite of the rest of the farmhouse.

I begin to remove the jars from the box and place them on the appropriate shelf. It's like a library of Mason jars. As I pull the last one out of the box, I feel something run across my bare foot. I shriek, yelling out as though I'd just been stabbed, and the glass container slips from my hand and crashes to the floor.

Globs of tomatoes, water, and shards of glass now cover my foot as I turn to run back into the kitchen. Running past the dining table, I race out to the back porch and start shaking my body, my hands rubbing across my arms and down my body to make sure nothing is on me.

"Yuck! Yuck! Yuck!" I yell.

I consider myself pretty tough, but I cannot do mice or rats or whatever it was that just scampered across my foot.

Gross!

Liam appears before me, winded. "Are you okay? I heard screaming," he says quickly before he pulls in a large breath.

"I'm fine. It was just—nothing." I nonchalantly wave my hand, the gesture contradictory to my racing heart. I'm not a wimp—or at least, he doesn't need to know that.

"Oh my God, Leni. Your foot!"

My eyes bulge when I look down to see my foot covered in blood. My adrenaline subsides, and I can feel the intense throbbing pain radiating from the top of my foot. The jar must have dropped right on it. In my frantic fight-or-flight reaction—where I clearly chose to run like hell—I didn't feel it.

Suddenly, I'm overcome with emotion—pain and sadness. I drop my chin to my chest, and I start to cry. I'm powerless to stop the tears now streaming down my cheeks.

I'm lifted off the ground as Liam takes me in his arms. I don't question it. I wrap my arms around his neck and bury my face against his shirt. One of his arms holds me under my knees, and my bloody foot swings as he walks somewhere.

I melt into him. My tears continue to fall, but now, they're quickly absorbed by his shirt. He smells amazing—an intoxicating mix of fabric softener, hay, and work. He feels so powerful and strong beneath my touch. I know I hate him for some reason, but right now, I need him.

He sets me up on a countertop.

I look around. I'm in a bathroom but not one in the farmhouse. "Where are we?"

"In the barn," he answers as he looks through a cupboard.

"No, we're not," I say, confused.

"I had a bathroom built out here after I bought the property. I spend more time here than I do at home, so it comes in handy." He pulls a big blue box with a red label that reads *First Aid Kit* out of the cupboard. "This is what I was looking for," he says to me with a kind smile. He wets a towel and starts to gently clean my foot. "So, what happened?"

"I dropped a jar of tomatoes on it."

Liam nods. "Must've hurt really bad. That was quite a scream."

"I actually didn't feel it hit my foot."

He brings his gaze up until he's looking directly at me, and his intense brown eyes stare at me in question. And, all at once, I don't care about any of it anymore—my need to seem tough or in control, my commitment to hating him, any of it. It's all just so stupid, and I'm so tired.

"Well, before I dropped the jar, a man-eating mouse ran across my foot. It was quite terrifying. My adrenaline must have been pumping through me in full force because I didn't realize I'd hurt my foot until you pointed it out."

"Man-eating?" Liam asks with a solemn nod. "Yeah, we've had quite the problem with those monstrous rodents around here lately. I saw a barn mouse yesterday, and I barely escaped with my life," he says seriously.

I can't help but laugh. "I'm not a fan of mice."

"Evidently." He grins back.

He focuses his attention back on my foot. I watch in awe as he takes such great care of me.

"Well, I don't think you need stitches. It's just a surface cut, and it should heal up fine. Sometimes, those surface ones are the biggest bleeders. You already have some bruising starting here though." He lightly traces his finger across my skin, and it causes me to shiver. After he bandages me all up, he hands me an ice pack. "This will help keep the swelling down."

"Thank you, Liam."

He raises his arm toward my face, and I hold my breath as I watch his hand get closer. With his thumb, he wipes the stray tears still resting beneath one of my eyes.

"You're welcome," he answers.

When he pulls his arm back, I'm able to breathe again. "You know, you don't have to be so nice to me. I don't deserve it."

"Whether or not that's true, it doesn't matter. You're a person who needed help. Of course I was going to help you. It's called being a good human being. I realize that you have built me up to be this awful person in your head, but I promise you, I'm not him."

He smiles, and as always, it says so much. He's such a good man. Besides Mimi, he's probably the kindest person I know.

Why have I always pushed him away?

Chalk it up to me being an emotional wreck, but I keep talking, "I know you're good, Liam. It's me who's the horrible one."

"You're not horrible, Len. You're just lost."

His words strike me deep, like a blow to my gut.

How does he see me so clearly?

He's right. I've been so lost for such a long time, and the harder I try to find myself, the further away I get.

My lip begins to tremble, and I will my tears to stay at bay. The sentence leaves my mouth before I can stop it. "I could really use a friend."

The corners of his mouth turn up into the most beautiful grin I've ever seen. "I told you, I can be a really good friend."

"Okay." I nod.

"Okay then." He lets out a content sigh.

He cleans up the bathroom while I sit on the counter, icing my foot.

"You know what I think you need?" he asks me.

"What's that?"

"A bonfire and beer. It's going to be cool tonight. It will be perfect."

"I don't like beer. It tastes like urine. Can we do a bonfire and martinis or a bonfire and wine?"

"Hell no. You're not in the big city anymore, sweetheart. We're doing beer, and I promise, you'll like it. You're not drinking the right beer if you think it tastes like piss. I'll get you the good stuff, okay?"

"Well, I'm not drinking any beer because it's gross. Can you bring a backup beverage just in case?" I ask with a smirk.

"I'll think about it." He shoots me a wink. "Hop on my back."

He turns around and leans back against the counter. I wrap my arms around his neck and my legs around his waist.

"I think my last piggyback ride was with you. We must have been … gosh, ten and eleven or so." I chuckle.

"Well, we can't have you hurting your foot, can we?" He leads us out of the barn and toward the house. "I'm going to take a quick shower, go grab some beer and food, and set the fire up. Then, I'll be back to get you, okay?"

"Sounds good. But can you do me a favor first?"

"Sure. What's up?"

"Can you please clean up the broken glass and tomatoes in the pantry? I don't want Mimi to step on it or anything, but I can't risk seeing that killer mouse again," I ask sheepishly.

Liam chuckles. "Yeah, I can do that."

"Thank you. You really are a good human being."

"Well, I try."

He leaves me on the couch before heading to the pantry. As he walks away, I smile wide. What a difference an hour makes in one's outlook on life. I don't feel so alone. I can't help but grin because I feel like things are starting to look up—well, that, and the fact that Liam's ass was made to wear those jeans.

nine

Liam

The fire blazes brightly. I have two coolers full of beer and food. I've hidden a bottle of wine underneath the sandwiches, just in case, but I really don't think Leni will need it. She doesn't think she'll like the beer, but I have confidence that she will. I've arranged bales of straw into a sofa-like seating area a safe distance from the bonfire. I covered the straw with a sheet so that Leni doesn't have to feel pieces of straw poking her back.

"Shit," I say into the night air.

This looks like a freaking date. It has a romantic vibe to it, and that's the last thing I need. I don't want to go and spook Leni. She's finally talking to me—and not just in insults.

It is what it is. Hopefully, she doesn't read too much into it. I mean, do I find Leni attractive? Hell yeah. She's the most beautiful woman I know. If she were anyone else that I had such a strong attraction to, I'd most definitely be fucking her on these bales of straw later. But she's not. She's my first best friend, the girl I spent most of my childhood summers with. She's finally my friend again, and she's hurting. I'd never do anything to add to her pain. She needs a friend, and that's what I'm going to be.

When I get up to the house, I see Mrs. Turner pulling some sheets off the clothesline. "Here, ma'am, let me help you with those."

"I'm just fine, Liam. But thank you. I can handle a little laundry. I like the work. My daddy always said that the moment you quit working is the moment you die." She chuckles. "He was a stubborn ole man all right. He did it though; he worked until the day he died. He was ninety-three."

"My granddaddy says the same thing." I grin. "Well, okay ... if you're sure."

She nods. "I'm sure. Besides, you have plans with my Leni girl. Thank you for not giving up on her. She comes from a long line of stubborn; it's not her fault."

I laugh because it's true. If Leni is anything, it's stubborn.

"You're welcome. I'm just glad she's talking to me again."

"Me, too. Me, too." Mrs. Turner nods her head. "She has me, of course, but that girl needs more friends her own age. I really do appreciate you being so patient with her, Liam. You're a good man."

"Thank you, ma'am."

I find Leni behind the house, rocking on the porch swing. "Hey you. You ready?"

"Yes." She stands from the swing, and when she does, she takes my breath away. She's wearing a flannel shirt that's tied at her waist, some form-fitting jeans, and cowboy boots.

Damn, she's sexy in boots.

Her hair is down, and it cascades over her shoulders in loose waves. She's a cowboy's dream.

"Wow, you look great."

"Thanks. I found this top and boots up in the closet. I think they might have belonged to Mimi at some point. Boots and flannels are pretty timeless, I suppose. I wanted to dress the part for our *bonfire and beer*." She says the last part with a southern twang, causing me to laugh. "I'm a Texas girl after all—at least for a little while until I figure out where to go and what to do."

"You'll always be a Texas girl, Len. You were born and raised here. You can take the girl out of Texas, but you ain't taking Texas out of the girl."

"I guess, but I haven't worn boots like this in years."

"Just like riding a bike." I wink. "Let's go."

We don't say much on the walk back to the field. There's an awkward air between us, but it is to be expected with our history. Today is the most we've spoken since I was seventeen. I'm not sure why it bothers me so much that we aren't friends anymore, but it really does. So much has changed over the past seven years, but at the same time, not much has really changed at all. I crave Leni's presence in my life more than I ever have. I guess I never really admitted how much her absence truly affected me. Just having her here these past couple of weeks has made my life more exciting. I wake up each day with a thrill of anticipation in hopes that today will be the day I get to see her.

"Wow, this looks awesome," Leni says when we reach the fire.

We take a seat on the straw-bale sofa. I reach into the cooler, grab a couple of beers, and pry off the metal caps.

"Here's the real test." I hand her a beer. "Keep an open mind. Remember, you can't compare it to a martini, Len. It's like comparing apples and oranges. Two separate things here."

"Okay. I'll drink it with an open mind."

I watch a little too intently as her lips close around the top of the bottle. She takes a long swig. She lowers the bottle from her mouth and smacks her lips together.

"Well?" I ask.

"It doesn't taste like urine," she says.

"And?"

She shrugs. "It's not bad. It's drinkable."

I chuckle. "You like it. Just admit it."

"You know I'm not going to let you be right," she says with a giggle, and it's the sweetest sound.

"Fair enough. I'll drop it. But I know the truth." I lean against what would be the arm of the sofa, if these bales of straw were indeed a giant sofa, so that I can look at Leni without cocking my head to the side.

The flicker from the firelight dances against her skin. I pull in a deep breath and remind myself that I'm just her friend. I have a feeling I'm going to have to repeat that mantra over again in my head quite a few times tonight.

Leni finishes her beer in record time, and I hand her another.

"What have you been up to since I last saw you, Liam?"

"You mean, since my seventeenth birthday when you told me that you never wanted to see me again?" I say before forcing out a small laugh.

"Yeah, that seems like a good place to start."

"Well, I spent that summer working with my dad on the ranch. Then, I finished my senior year of high school. Worked another summer on the ranch before leaving for college. I went to Texas A&M and got a degree in agricultural business. I came home every summer and helped my dad. College was great. Lots of fun, too much drinking. The norm. Then, after college, I came home and bought your grandma's ranch. I have been working the land and trying to build up the cattle numbers ever since. Nothing shocking."

"So, no secret marriages or offspring in there anywhere?"

I laugh. "Definitely not."

"Did you date in college? Any serious relationships?"

"Yeah, sure, I dated. Some more serious than others. None of them worth bringing home though."

Leni asks more questions about my time at college, and I answer. She can ask me anything. I'm just so relieved we're talking.

I throw some more wood on the fire, and Leni insists that we play a drinking game called Never Have I Ever. The concept seems pretty straightforward.

As soon as she asks the first question, I realize how very dangerous this drinking game can be.

"Never have I ever had a threesome," she states easily.

I almost choke on the gulp of beer that I was taking. "What kind of game is this, Len? Jeez."

She laughs. "It's simple. If you've never had a threesome, then it's your turn to say something you've never done. If you've had a threesome, you need to chug your beer until it's gone."

"Well ... I don't think I have," I state cautiously.

She playfully hits my shoulder. "Don't you skirt around this one, William Moore. You'd know whether you had one or not."

"What constitutes a threesome?" I ask.

"Have you been naked or semi-naked with more than one person before?"

I shrug. "Yeah, but I didn't have sex with both of them."

"Two other girls?" she inquires.

My eyes widen. "Yes, of course, two girls."

"Did you kiss both of them and touch their boobs or other parts? Or did they both touch you?"

"Jesus, Len!"

A day ago, she wasn't talking to me, and now, she's asking me this.

"Answer the question, mister."

"There was some touching, I guess ... but it wasn't like a porno movie. I'm not a bad guy. It was at one of our house parties. We were all very drunk," I explain.

"I don't think you're a bad guy, Liam. Threesomes aren't that uncommon." She giggles. "So, based on what you've told me, I need you to down that bottle of beer and get a new one." She throws me a wink.

I do as she said and ask, "This is what you did for fun in New York?"

"We played a few times." She grins. "Your turn."

"Okay. Um ... never have I ever kissed a guy."

She throws her head back in laughter. "That is so lame, Liam. You know I have."

I nod, a sly grin on my face. "That I do. Now, chug it, baby."

The game continues, and I quickly realize that the purpose of the game is to get your opponent drunk as quickly as possible. How one actually wins ... I haven't figured out.

"Never have I ever had sex in the bed of a pickup truck."

I down a beer.

"Never have I ever seen the Statue of Liberty in person."

She downs a beer.

"Never have I ever had sex with someone who attended Texas A&M."

I drink.

"Never have I ever made a sculpture."

She drinks.

"Never have I ever gone down on a girl."

I chug.

"Never have I ever almost gotten hit by a truck while crossing the street."

She chugs.

All her questions are of a sexual nature, but I can't make myself go there with her. I still feel like I'm walking on eggshells, terrified of saying something wrong and driving her away.

"Never have I ever been in love," she says.

I stare into her eyes. I don't drink my beer this time.

"You've never been in love?" she asks quietly.

"I don't think so. I've loved, but *in love* is different, right?"

She nods. "Yeah, I think it is."

"So, you haven't either?" I ask her though I know the answer since she's the one who made the statement.

"I don't think so. What do you think the main difference is between the two?" she questions.

"I'm not entirely sure. But I'd say that, if you were in love with someone, the feeling would be reciprocated. Don't you think?"

"Yeah, that makes sense."

Thanks to Leni's game, we've both drunk way more beer than we probably should have. But I wonder if maybe she needed it to open up.

"Tell me about New York. Was it everything you wanted it to be?"

She thinks for a minute before answering, "It was great. So unlike here. It truly is like a completely different world, living there. The first month or so was pretty overwhelming. There are tons of people. Everyone's always in a hurry. The first few weeks, it was hard to catch my breath. But, after a bit, I got into the flow of the city. All the busyness, the noise, the movements—there's a cadence to it. You know? Once I figured out my rhythm, it was pretty awesome."

"College was good?"

"College was the best. My professors were incredible. I learned so much, and it was special, being around those who loved art as much as I did."

"And your friends?"

"I had a lot of friends. I really did." She pauses and watches the fire for a moment. "I guess I thought my friendships were real, and maybe they were, but they were also shallow, too. It's hard to explain. There are those people in your life who are meant to be there for a while. They have a certain purpose, specific to a time in your life. Then, you have your forever friends—the people who are in it for the long haul, no matter the circumstances. Now that I'm here, I realize they weren't the latter. Truthfully, I don't have any true lifelong friends."

She shakes her head, and her face wears a sorrowful expression. "I don't know how I got here, to this place where I don't have anyone besides Mimi. I should have more at this point. I've been trying so hard, but I'm failing. There comes a point where I can't keep blaming everyone else, and I have to stop and wonder what's wrong with me."

"You have me," I tell her.

She turns her head, giving me a sad smile. "I don't deserve you."

"Well, that's neither here nor there because you have me. Always have, always will … my Leni girl."

We both turn to face the flames of the fire. Leni leans her head against my shoulder. I wrap my arm around her and pull her close.

"Are you happier here?" I ask.

She shrugs her shoulders. "I love being with Mimi, and I'm glad we're friends again. But I'm just unhappy."

"Do your art. That always made you happy. Paint a picture or something."

"I sold all my stuff to one of my roommates. Hundreds of dollars in supplies, and she got it all for fifty dollars." She sighs. "Desperate times."

"Well, that sucks."

"Yeah," she agrees. "It's weird, being friends with adult Liam."

"Why's that?" I chuckle.

"Our conversations are so deep. Grown-up Liam and Leni are kinda downers—or at least, I am. We were cooler at eleven and twelve."

"I was not cooler at twelve. God, that was an awkward year." I think back. "And eleven-year-old Leni would have washed her own mouth out with soap after that game of Never Have I Ever."

"Ha! True. Grown-up Leni has some perks."

"Definite perks."

Leni turns her face toward mine. She's so close; I'm afraid she's going to hear my heart pounding in my chest.

"Thank you for tonight. This Texas thing isn't completely bad."

"Leni love, it is now my mission as your newly reappointed best friend to make you fall in love"—her breath hitches, and she leans in closer—"with Texas again," I finish my thought though it's hard to focus on anything but her plump lips. I've dreamed of her lips more times than I can count.

Our faces are an inch apart, and my chest aches with the closeness. She's even more beautiful by firelight. Regardless of what happens tomorrow, even if she decides to hate me again, I'll have this memory of tonight. And, as far as nights go, it's been pretty great.

"Len ..." My voice is strained.

"Yeah?" she answers breathlessly and closes her eyes.

I imagine running my fingers through her hair and pulling her lips against mine, but I can't. Not like this.

She needs a friend, I remind myself.

"I should walk you back," I say on an exhale.

Her eyes snap open. "Oh, yeah. Okay. You're probably right. My head's kinda foggy."

"Well, you can blame that feeling on your brilliant drinking game," I tease as we start walking back toward the farmhouse.

She wraps her arm through mine and leans against me as we walk.

Right before she heads inside the house, I ask, "Len?"

"Yeah?"

"Can you promise me one thing?"

"What's that?"

"Please don't hate me again tomorrow."

My request causes her lips to pout out.

She pins me with a serious stare. "I won't."

And, as she closes the door behind her, I really want to believe her.

ten

Leni

It's been a little over a week since the bonfire with Liam, and I'd be lying if I said my outlook on life hasn't improved since then. Nothing has really changed, but in a way, so much has. I just feel lighter, less burdened, and freer. Holding on to a grudge, especially one that isn't warranted, is exhausting.

I haven't really hung out with Liam since that night. He's been busy working the farm and traveling to buy cows or something. I'm still not well versed in the life of a rancher. I'm not sure exactly what he's doing, but it requires him to be away from the ranch a lot. But I have been able to see him a few times. We've waved and exchanged pleasantries, and I've brought him out some cold sweet tea on a couple of occasions.

I think I'm just happy because we're friends again, and unlike my friends from New York, Liam's as real as they come.

As Mimi always says, "That boy has a heart of gold."

If being on the ranch offers me anything, it's time to think. Self-reflection has become my full-time job, and truthfully, I need it.

I've made peace with the fact that the relationships I built in the city weren't what I thought they were. I'd rather have one real friend than a hundred fake ones. A true friend, one like Liam, knows all my imperfections and loves me anyway. And, Lord knows, I've got my fair share of imperfections.

There's a knock on the front door. I close the *Southern Living* magazine I was reading. It's desperate times for entertainment here. There isn't much I want to do at Mimi's, so learning how to make the perfect lattice pie crust for an apple pie is as good as it gets at the moment.

Opening the door, I find Liam.

"Hey," I greet him.

Seeing him standing outside the door on Mimi's front porch brings back so many memories of finding him in this exact spot over a span of years during my childhood. I can picture him in his muddy shorts, holding a frog, when he didn't have most of his front teeth. I can remember him here at the age of eight, holding fishing poles with his hair sticking up in random spots. There was the summer he greeted me with a giant bag of cotton candy he had gotten at the carnival. I remember him then holding the huge bag of fluffed sugar at the age of twelve when his nose was a little too big for his face. I remember them all because my friendship with Liam was the best thing about my childhood.

And he's here now—a handsome grown man with a college degree, a ranch, and his own business. So much has changed, and yet he still wears a wide grin as he holds up a brown mystery bag.

"What's in the bag?" I say slowly with a chuckle.

He bites his bottom lip before saying with a sneaky grin, "One word: Pablo's."

I gasp, bringing my hands up to my mouth. "Pablo's Tacos!"

"The one and only, just the way you like them—with extra onions and cilantro."

"Oh my gosh! I can't believe Pablo's is still around, and I can't believe you remember little details like that." I shake my head, my lips turning up in a grin.

"Like what? That you love your onions and cilantro with a side of taco?"

I chuckle. "Yeah, like that."

He presses his lips together and thoughtfully peers at me. "I remember everything about you, Leni."

There's a familiar pressure in my chest. I haven't felt it in so long, but every time I have, I've been in Liam's presence. It makes me pause because I don't want it to be there, yet when Liam's involved, sometimes, I don't have a choice.

Don't freak out. You need a friend.

I remind myself of the fact that having a real friend is important. Right now, I need Liam more than I need to run.

"You okay?" Liam's voice breaks my thoughts.

I shake my head. "Yeah, just thinking."

His gaze is apprehensive. "Good. Well, I don't know if you remember, but the last time we ate Pablo's together, we were at the drive-in."

"Yes! Watching that horrible movie about—what was it? Robots taking over and stealing our lives?"

He laughs. "That was it. I don't even remember the title, but even at thirteen, I knew it was shit."

"Remember the robot ball where they were all waltzing very awkwardly?" I giggle.

"How could I forget? Dumbest scene ever." He shakes his head. "Well, anyway, I was thinking it might be fun to go to the drive-in, watch a movie, and eat some tacos? What do you say?"

"Um, yeah. But"—I look back toward the kitchen—"Mimi's been in there, cooking something up, for a while now. I should probably eat dinner here."

From out of nowhere, Mimi shows up behind me. "Don't you worry yourself. You go on and have fun."

"You've been working so hard on dinner. I don't want your food to go to waste," I tell her.

She dismissively waves her hand through the air and shakes her head. "You don't have to worry about that. It won't. My friend Ana from church broke her arm yesterday. I'm going to package up this meal and take it to her. I'm sure her family will enjoy it."

"Oh, that's so nice. I'm positive they will love it. Okay. Well, if you're sure?"

"I'm sure." She pushes me toward the door. "Go. Have fun."

I toss the magazine onto the sofa and follow Liam out to his truck after giving Mimi a hug.

"I feel like Mimi is trying to get rid of me," I kid. "She was so eager to get me out of the house," I say to Liam as we walk toward his truck.

"Well, can you blame her? Was that a *Southern Living* magazine I saw you holding?" He chuckles, getting into the truck.

"Hey," I protest, closing the passenger door of the vehicle and buckling my seat belt. "It's not like she has a copy of *Fifty Shades of Grey* lying around. The pickings are slim."

"What's the shades of gray?"

"*Fifty Shades of Grey*? Like, the most popular romance novel of all time? You've never heard of it?"

"Can't say I have."

I shake my head and scoff under my breath.

"What?" Liam asks.

"This place is so sheltered—Elkwood, I mean."

"I don't think it's this place, Len. It's me. I'm not much into the romance-novel scene."

I stare out the window as we pass miles of cornfields. "Yeah, well, they're kind of a big deal—those books. There are movies and everything."

"Maybe one will be playing tonight?" he says.

I laugh.

How awkward would watching one of those movies with Liam be?

"No. They're all out on Blu-ray already. But, speaking of movies, I brought up that robot movie with my friends from college, and no one that I encountered had ever seen it before."

The truck slows as we approach our destination. "Yeah, well, I don't think it was a real movie."

"What do you mean?"

"Anyone with money can make a movie, and you can pay any theater to show it. I think some Texan with a lot of cash decided to take his shot as a movie producer and failed."

"Really?"

"Yeah. I had a friend in college who made this amateur scary movie, like *Blair Witch*–style. Then, he rented out the theater for its premiere."

"Did he sell tickets?" I wonder.

"Oh, yeah. He almost filled the theater. Granted, many of the moviegoers wanted refunds." Liam laughs. "I don't think everyone who paid for tickets realized what they were paying for."

"Oh my gosh. That's hilarious."

"It really was. It was a great night."

Liam pulls into the drive-in parking lot and backs up, so the bed of the truck is facing the screen. Being with Liam like this, as friends, is the most joy I've felt since being back. It's nice to chat about stuff that doesn't mean anything. It gives me a break from the heavy questions— like, *What are you doing with your life?* The sadness is still there, but hanging out with Liam is giving me a much-needed reprieve from dwelling on it.

He sets up two camping chairs in the bed of the truck. In between the two chairs is a basket of goodies— chips, candy, and popcorn. He produces a cooler from the backseat of the truck and sets that in front of the chairs as well. Sometimes, it's hard to hang out with Liam because he's always this sweet and over-the-top wonderful. He always has been. As much as I love the setup and can't believe how perfect it is, it makes me feel guilty for all of the horrible things I've put him through in my life. I'm really trying not to focus on the past because what's done is done, but then he goes and does something so thoughtful, and it fills me with remorse.

"This is really sweet," I tell him, my voice a whisper.

He raises an eyebrow. "Then, why do you sound like that?"

"Honestly?"

He nods.

"You being so nice to me makes me feel bad because I don't deserve it, Liam. I don't. I've been miserable toward you."

"None of that matters now. You have to get out of your head, Leni. You're stuck in regrets, the past, and things you can't change. I don't care what was or wasn't said when we were kids. We're adults now, and we can make different choices. Right?"

"Yeah," I agree.

"Okay, then stop. You were once my best friend, and I've missed you. That's all there is to it. None of the other stuff makes a difference now." He opens the cooler and waves his hand in front of it, Vanna White–style, causing me to laugh.

Then, I gasp when I see the contents. There are bottles of Grape Crush sitting atop ice. "Grape!"

"Your favorite." He grins.

I think back to all the times that Liam and I argued over which was better—orange or grape soda. "Where's the orange?" I ask.

He smiles. "I always liked grape better, too. I just said orange to be different, to have something to argue with you about."

I shoot him a wink. "I told you grape was better."

We sit down in the chairs with our sodas and tacos. It'll be a little while before the movie starts, as they wait until it's completely dark.

I take a big bite of a taco and hum in contentment as I roll my eyes back into my head. "Oh, yes."

"As good as you remember?" Liam asks.

"Definitely. You know, as diverse as New York is and as many authentic Mexican food places as there are, I never found tacos that held a candle to Pablo's." I look around at all the parked cars and people setting up for their movie. "I'm surprised this place is still open. I feel like most of the drive-ins have closed down."

"Yeah, there's not many left," Liam agrees. "This one sure brings back memories though."

"It sure does. Mimi was so sweet. She would drive us and then just sit in the car and crochet. The audio from the movie blared so loudly through the speakers, so we could hear it in our chairs outside. That must have hurt her ears. I never thought about it back then. I wonder why she brought us every week."

"Because she loves you and knew you loved coming here," Liam states.

"Yeah."

Liam's right. Mimi does love me. I'm so fortunate to have her. Truthfully, I don't know where I'd be if I didn't. Not everyone has a perfect, loving family. Many aren't supported by the ones who should love them most. I'm not unique in that aspect of my life. But everyone needs at least one person to love them unconditionally, one person to show them that they are worthy of a good life. Mimi has always been that person for me. I have too many flaws to count, but everything that's good in me is a direct result of Mimi's love.

I turn to Liam and can't help but think that he's my person, too—or he would've been had I not pushed him away. He was always there for me, just as he's here for me now.

"What?" He raises an eyebrow in question. "What are you thinking?"

"Nothing." I shrug.

"No, you're making your face. There's something on your mind."

I grin. "What face?"

"The one you make when you're contemplating something important."

I tap him on his arm. "I do not make a face."

"Oh, but you do." He chuckles. "What is it? Tell me."

"Fine. I was just thinking about how very much I love tacos."

My response elicits laughter from Liam, and the sound fills my soul with a contentment that I haven't felt in so long.

"I don't know if I buy that, but I'll accept it." He gives me a wink.

I want to tell Liam how thankful I am that he's being so kind to me when I've done nothing to deserve it. I want to tell him how much I appreciate him hanging out with me when I'm such a downer. I want to tell him so many things, but I can't. I have no idea what tomorrow will bring. My emotions are on a teeter-totter from hell. When they're up, it's awesome. But then they fall without warning, suddenly hitting the ground hard. As much as I want to hope that I'll stay up here where life is good, I know the floor is just beneath me, bracing for my inevitable impact.

What goes up must come down, and I will. I always do.

I just don't want to crush Liam in the process.

eleven

Leni

*P*ain shoots through my fingers, and I cringe. "How do you do this without your hands aching?" I ask Mimi as I knead the ball of bread dough.

Mimi has decided to teach me how to make her famous bread, reminding me that she won't be here forever—a thought that I refuse to think about.

"You get used to it." She chuckles.

I feel like a major wimp because my hands seriously hurt. "How is it that my grandmother is more badass than I am?" I shake my head with a laugh.

"You got soft up there in the Big Apple, sweetie. You'll toughen up after you've been here for a while," she says as she works on the opposite counter, pounding some chicken breasts flat.

"Mimi, what should I do with my life? I can't just stay here forever."

"Of course you can. You're always welcome here."

"I know that, but I'm not *doing* anything, you know? I have a fancy degree. I should be using it." I start to pound the dough with my fists to get the air bubbles out because this kneading crap is killing my knuckles.

"Why don't we go into town for some dessert? We can stop off at the library beforehand, and you can do some job-searching on the internet. I'm sure there's plenty you could be doing. Maybe you could teach some classes at a nearby community college," she recommends as she dips the flattened chicken in a flour mixture.

"Okay, that sounds great. Where are we going for dessert?"

My appetite has tripled since I've been in Texas, and with the mention of dessert, I'm now craving something sweet. I can't stop myself from eating; it's a problem. Mimi's cooking is the best thing in the world, but it's also the devil.

"Let's go to Franny's Kitchen," Mimi suggests. "Do you remember Franny's Kitchen?"

"Oh my goodness … Franny's Kitchen! Of course I remember. I think the French toast there is one of the most delicious things I've ever put in my mouth."

Mimi laughs. "You've been saying that a lot lately."

"Well, it's true. A few more weeks of this, and I won't fit into my clothes any longer." I push out my belly and blow air into my cheeks. I dramatically pat my stomach.

"You are many things, my love, but chubby isn't one of them. In fact, you could stand to put on ten pounds or so. You got too skinny up there in New York. I don't know what you were eating, but it wasn't enough," Mimi says.

"I was eating plenty, and I'm perfectly healthy. I promise you, I don't *need* to put on weight, though I have a feeling that whether or not I need to is irrelevant while living here. I think a weight gain is inevitable." I tilt my head toward the bowl of dough.

Mimi just shakes her head with a small grin.

I portion out the dough and put them into bread pans before covering the loaf pans with a towel while they rise. After I wash my hands, I step behind Mimi and wrap my arms around her. "I promise to eat less bread."

"Why's that?"

"Because, now, I know how hard it is to make."

Mimi chuckles again. "You eat all the bread you want, Leni girl. I don't mind making more." She wipes her floured hands against her apron. "Would you mind grabbing the mail?"

"Sure."

I give Mimi one more squeeze and then make my way through the living room. I open the front door and gasp, bringing my hands to my mouth.

"What is it?" Mimi calls from the kitchen.

I can't answer though because I'm utterly speechless

My chest fills with so much emotion that I can't contain it all, and it escapes in the form of tears.

Oh my gosh. Unbelievable.

"Well, I'll be," Mimi says, now standing beside me. "I told ya, heart o' gold."

She retreats back to the kitchen and leaves me staring at one of the nicest things anyone has ever done for me.

Covering a large portion of the front porch are baskets stocked full of art supplies. I step outside and slowly walk around the treasures, my fingers swiping over everything. This is better than all the Christmas mornings I had as a child. I think anything I could possibly need is here—an easel, all types of paint, palettes, brushes, sketchpads, colored pencils, chalk, clay, tools, finishes, and canvases. It's enough to fully stock an art studio. And it's good stuff, too. These paintbrushes aren't from the local craft store; these are the brushes professionals use. He had to have gotten all this somewhere outside of Elkwood, maybe in Austin.

I look around for a card, and I find it in one of the baskets. It's a simple card with a picture of a Texas skyline at sunset. Inside is a handwritten note.

Be happy.
—Liam

I bring the card to my chest and hug it tight, pulling in a big breath of air. Tears continue to roll down my cheeks, but I don't care to stop them. I can't remember the last time I cried because I was so overcome with joy.

Has there ever been a time?

I sit cross-legged on the porch and go through each basket, reading the labels on each item.

Oh my gosh, I have to paint!

I hop up and run inside, one of the huge baskets of goodies in my arms.

"Mimi, can I turn one of the bedrooms into an art studio?"

"Of course, dear. Go for it." She motions up toward the bedrooms.

"Thank you!" I bounce up and down on the balls of my feet. "Can we run into town another day?"

Mimi smiles wide. "Absolutely. Have fun, sweet girl."

I choose the bedroom with the most windows. I work up a sweat, rearranging the room. I'm so excited to get to the art part that I basically just push everything up against one wall, so I can have an open space to set up the easel.

I yell downstairs, "Mimi, can I use some of these top sheets in the closet as tarps?" I don't want to ruin her wood floors.

"Yes!" she calls up.

"You know that they'll be ruined with paint, right?" I double-check with her.

"Absolutely have at it," she says loudly from the kitchen.

"Okay. Do you want to tell me which ones to use?" At this point, I should probably just run downstairs and have an actual conversation with her, but I'm too excited to take the time.

"Nope. They're all fair game."

I clap my hands together and pull a pile of sheets from the linen closet.

When the room is ready, I start bringing everything in and setting it up. It's an amateur job, but I can spend more time organizing it all later. Right now, I need to just get to it.

I run to my room to grab my iPod and put my headphones on. Finally, with a brush in hand, music playing, I swipe beautiful colors across a canvas.

Nothing has ever made me as happy as art does. I feel I was born to create, to push boundaries, to be different. I wasn't made to conform but to stand out.

When other girls my age asked for dolls, I asked for a pottery wheel. When the same-age girls in our social circle were training to be ladies and performing in pageants, all I wanted to do was learn how to perfectly capture a horse's beauty, using oil-based paints.

My parents humored my creative fascination for a while, though it was a continuous topic of contention in our home. I think they blamed my *projects* for the fact that I would argue, complain, and act out every time I was forced to attend a function where I was told to be someone other than myself. But it wasn't the art that made me behave that way. It was them and the life I was forced to live. They never cared if I was happy, only that I acted the part when I was told to do so.

What they never understood was that art was my therapy, my saving grace in a life that was trying to smother me at every turn. I could fake it when I had to as long as I had an outlet. But, when I was thirteen, they took my happiness away.

Looking back, it's so absurd. What parent would forbid their child to complete art projects?

After a particularly bad fight with my father, he had everything in my art studio thrown out. I think it was then that I realized my parents were never going to love me. To truly love me, they'd have to make an attempt to know me, to understand me. But they hadn't. I would always be the daughter who wasn't good enough. But thank God for Mimi, my innate self-pride, and my intense stubbornness because my parents didn't break me. They only made me fight harder.

I never completed another art piece at home, but I took as many art classes in school as I could. I would stay late almost every day, telling my parents that I had study groups when, in reality, I was working with Mr. Shillaci, the art teacher. He would spend countless hours teaching me new techniques and mentoring me so that I could get into one of the best college art programs.

I know that hours have gone by based on where I am in my playlist, but I have no desire to stop. At all. Missing Mimi's dinner and dessert at Franny's Kitchen doesn't even cause me to pause. I still have no idea of where I'm going or what I'm doing with my life, yet I no longer feel stressed about it.

I stop painting for a moment and take in the canvas before me. I really hadn't thought about what I was going to create; it just happened. Sitting here now might be the happiest I've been in years. I have to shake my head and laugh because, out of infinite options for my first piece with all my new goodies, I ended up painting Texas. And not just a generic Texas picture, but of Mimi's backyard—the barn, the rolling hills of the pasture, and the endless horizon at twilight full of captivating hues of pink, orange, and yellow. The piece of art has a dreamy quality to it, the layers of paint rising from the canvas giving a real-life feeling, as if I could just step into the picture and explore.

This view used to make me feel trapped and anxious to escape this state and life, but it brings different sensations now. I can hardly understand it, but at this moment, when I see the stunning landscape before me, my heart fills with gratitude, hope, and genuine joy.

twelve

Liam

I wipe my hands on my jeans as I walk up to Mrs. Turner's house. It's been days since I dropped off Leni's surprise, and I'm so anxious to see how she liked it. She left a couple messages on my phone, telling me to call her, and she sounded truly happy. Yet I've been so busy with helping my dad move cattle this past week that I've hardly been able to spend any time on my land.

I gently rap on the screen door, and Mrs. Turner opens it up for me.

"Morning, ma'am. Is Leni available?" I ask.

"She sure is," she says with a smile. "She's up in the studio."

"The studio?"

"Oh, yeah. She did some rearranging after your generous gifts. Has barely come down to eat in three days." She takes my hand in hers and squeezes. "Thank you, Liam."

"It was nothing."

She shakes her head. "No, it was a whole lot of something. Thank you."

I smile to her and head toward the steps leading up to the bedrooms.

"Liam?"

"Yes, ma'am?"

"Maybe try to get her to get out for a bit. I know she's in her little paradise up there, but the girl has to eat."

I chuckle. "Will do."

I follow Leni's humming to one of the bedrooms. The door is open, and I peek in. My heart swells at the sight of her. I lean against the doorframe to take her in. She's in short shorts and a tank top. Her hair is pulled high on her head in a messy bun. She's humming to some song that is playing through her headphones, though I can't make out what song it is. She is sitting on a chair in front of a canvas and painting. She radiates happiness, and the vision of her this content is utterly mesmerizing.

After a bit, she must feel my stare because she looks over her shoulder. Her smile goes wide when she sees me. She drops her paintbrush and rips the headphones from her head as she runs over to me. Throwing her arms around me, she pulls me into a hug as she squeals loudly.

"Liam! Thank you! Thank you! Thank you!" she says into my neck.

I hug her back and kiss the top of her head. "You're welcome. I'm so glad you like everything."

"Oh my God, I love everything! This is the nicest thing anyone has ever done for me. It had to cost a fortune. I don't know how to repay you."

"No repayment necessary. It's a gift, Len. I did it because I wanted to. I don't expect anything in return." I stare into her green eyes that appear to shine brighter today.

She has some errant loose, wispy locks of hair that fell from her bun, framing her face. She isn't wearing an ounce of makeup and looks so innocent. I tuck one of the pieces of hair behind her ear. She has a smear of white paint across her nose, and it's so goddamn sexy. In fact, this entire look that she has going on is hot as hell.

"Are you happy?" I ask the only question that really matters.

"So happy. I didn't understand how much my art brings me to life. I missed it more than I realized."

"Happiness looks real good on you, Len. Real good."

She releases her arms from around my waist. "Oh, I have something for you!" She skips over to a pile of completed pieces.

I follow her into the room.

"So, I know it's not much, compared to what you did for me, but I made you something." She hands me a large canvas. "It's the very first painting I did."

In my hands, I hold a painting of the farm. I love it here and think this land is stunning. Yet this painting makes it even more so. The way she blends colors and textures together ... it's fascinating. At a distance, the barn looks like a typical barn red shade, but at closer look, I can see strokes of different shades of reds and browns that she used to get the final color. The entire painting rises off of the canvas from layers of perfectly placed hues. The rolling hills behind the house are so enchanting that my stare gets lost in them. For a minute, I'm speechless.

"You're really, really good," I finally manage to say.

"So, you like it?" She stares up to me with an expectant smile.

"I love it. It's amazing."

"I thought you would like it for your house someday." She shrugs.

"Absolutely. This beauty needs a proper frame, and then it's going up on the wall."

"Yay! Great."

"Can I see what else you've done?" I ask.

"Absolutely!"

Leni shows me her other paintings, and they're all equally as captivating. I don't know a lot about art, but I know that Leni has some serious talent. I have no idea why her pieces didn't sell up north because they're better than any painting I've ever seen.

After she's done showing me her work, I ask, "So, what are you up to today?"

"Just this." She shrugs, pointing to the easel.

"Well, actually, I would like you to repay me for everything."

She flinches slightly and looks confused. "Um ... okay ... I'll have to—"

"I don't want any money," I clarify. "I want to take you to town to eat."

She puts her hands on her hips and squints her eyes toward me. "You want me to repay you for all this awesomeness by allowing you to take me to get some food?"

"Yep. Those are my terms."

She shakes her head with a laugh. "Okay. I suppose a girl's gotta do what a girl's gotta do."

She's so incredibly fascinating; I can hardly think straight around her.

I step toward her. Without thinking it through, I lick my thumb and wipe it against the paint on her nose. Her eyes go wide. My heart races as my thumb glides across her skin. I slowly drop my hand and allow my thumb to slide over her lips. Her sharp intake of breath halts my action, and I pull my hand away.

I clear my throat. "You had paint ... on your ..." I do a circular motion in front of her face. My mouth suddenly feels dry, and I swallow.

She takes a second. "So, the best course of action was to rub your spit on me?" she says, breaking the awkward tension.

I laugh and move a step back from her. "Yeah, not my best move."

"Probably not." She winks. "Let me go get cleaned up really quick."

Twenty minutes later, we're in my truck, heading to Franny's Kitchen diner in town. The air around us is light and carefree—a complete one-eighty from the last time I had Leni in my truck.

"Hungry?" I laugh as Leni shovels French toast into her mouth.

"Oh my gosh ... yes! I didn't even realize I was so hungry. I guess I've been kind of obsessed with my new studio the last few days. I haven't eaten as much as usual." She grabs a napkin and wipes her mouth.

"It's awesome that you're in your little artist world ... but you still have to participate in life. Stuff, like eating, is kind of important." I lean back in the booth and shoot her a smirk.

She playfully rolls her eyes. "I know. I'll be better." She finishes her plate and puts some cream in her coffee. "I love this place. It reminds me of my summers with Mimi. We'd come a couple of times a week for breakfast."

"Franny's Kitchen definitely has the best breakfast menu."

The bell atop the door jingles, and my friend Pete and his very pregnant wife, Melody, walk into the diner. Pete notices me and heads over to our table, holding Melody's hand, who very cutely hobbles behind him.

"Hey, man," he says to me.

"Hey, Pete, Melody," I greet them both. "This is my friend Leni," I introduce them. "She's Mrs. Turner's granddaughter. She just moved back from New York."

"Oh, yeah. Emma said something about Mrs. Turner's granddaughter coming back to stay," Melody says.

Leni looks up to her in question.

"There isn't a lot of exciting gossip in this town. You moving back was big news. Your grandma talks about you every time I see her. Don't worry; it's all good things. She's very proud of you." She smiles at Leni.

"It's nice to meet you." Leni smiles. "When are you due?"

Melody rubs her belly with her free hand. "Next month. I can't wait."

"Do you know what you're having?" Leni asks.

"Nope. We're going to be surprised." Melody grins wide.

"This week, we feel like the little one is a boy, but next week, he'll probably be back to a girl." Pete chuckles before addressing me, "Did you and your dad get all the cattle moved? Did you get a good price?"

"Yeah, it was a long week, but we're done. We did really well. I can't complain," I answer.

"You ready to get started on your house?" Pete asks.

I smile. "Not yet, man. Soon. I'll let you know."

"Okay, sounds good. Looking forward to it." He faces his wife, and they exchange a sweet look before he kisses her on the top of her head. He turns back toward the table. "Well, it was a pleasure meeting you, Leni. I've gotta go get my wife some food. She's having some serious Franny's Kitchen cravings, and what my sweetheart wants, she gets." He winks toward Melody.

"It was nice meeting you," Leni says. "And good luck with the baby."

"Thanks," Melody says.

"Call me about your house," Pete says to me again.

"I will. See ya."

We watch as they make their way to a booth. Pete gets Melody situated on her side of the table before taking a seat.

"They seem nice," Leni says.

"Yeah, they're good people. Pete actually went to Texas A&M as well. I didn't really know him then. He moved back to Elkwood after college and runs his grandfather's ranch now. He's helped my dad and me out some and vice versa."

"He's really sweet to his wife. What's in the water here? You guys are so nice, nothing like the guys I dated in the city."

I hate to think of her dating other guys. "You couldn't have dated any decent ones then. It's just normal to be sweet to your girl when you love her."

"Huh." She looks at me with an odd expression. "So, what house plans was he talking about?"

"He's an architect. He designed the house he and Melody live in. He's going to design mine when I'm ready to get to building it."

"You're building a house?" she asks.

"Yeah, I'm hoping your grandma will be around for a long time, so her house isn't available, and I don't want to live with my parents forever." I chuckle. "I had a small room and bathroom built in the barn since I'm there so much. So, I stay there sometimes. But, eventually, I want to build my own place … somewhere on the property."

"What are you waiting for?" she asks.

"I'm not really sure. It just doesn't seem like the time."

I don't tell Leni, but truthfully, I don't see the point of building a big, new house right now if I'm the only one who's going to be living there. I don't need much, and the room in the barn is plenty sufficient for me.

Leni nods in understanding. "Well, if I'm still here when you do, maybe I can help you decorate. I took some interior design classes in college, and I have an eye for it. It would be fun."

"Absolutely. I have no doubt that you're great at that sort of thing. I, on the other hand, suck at it."

"Speaking of people our age who are married with babies on the way, did I tell you I hung out with Emily a couple of weeks ago? Did you know that she's, like, six months pregnant?" Leni asks, evident panic in her voice.

I laugh. "Yeah, I knew. Westley told me shortly after they found out. You're not a fan of being married with a kid on the way?"

"God, no," she admits. "I'm still trying to figure out my own life. I can't imagine taking care of someone else. Poor baby."

I chuckle. "Well, they're happy. Plus, they've been together for what, like eight years?"

"Yeah, since Emily and I were sophomores in high school. It's crazy that two people my age can know exactly what they want in life when I don't know what I'll be doing next week." She shakes her head. "I'm happy for them though. I mean, Emily's like over-the-moon ecstatic about her life. So, who am I to judge?"

Her statement elicits more laughter from me. "Look at you. You get a little painting time in, and you're all about the self-discovery. Who is this Leni, and where's the moody, judgmental girl I know?"

She throws her napkin at me. "Hey, you said that you know I'm not truly those things. I'm trying. Okay?"

"I know you're not, and I see that you are. I'm glad."

Glad is an understatement. The girl sitting across the table from me now and the girl I almost hit with my truck a few weeks ago are vastly different. Leni hasn't completely let go of everything that's been holding her down, but she's getting there. She's right; she's definitely trying.

We finish our meal, I pay, and we head out to the truck. The conversation is light on the way back to the farm.

"So, ranch work has slowed down a bit for you?" Leni asks.

"There's no shortage of work to be done. But I'll be around more, if that's what you mean."

"Yeah, that's what I meant. Well, that's good. I think I'm going to go into town someday this week and see what jobs there are to apply to. I can't just mooch off of Mimi forever." Her arm is hanging outside the open passenger window as she waves her hand through the air.

"I guarantee you that Mimi doesn't think you're mooching. I know she loves having you there," I tell her.

"Oh, I know she does. But, still … I have to do something. I'm no longer a child, and this isn't summer break. I have to contribute somehow." Her hand goes up and down through the outside air, making a wave-like motion.

The words come out of my mouth before I really think about them, "You could come and work for me."

What? What in the hell could Leni do on the ranch?

"Really? What could I do for you on the ranch? I don't know anything about that type of stuff." Her concerns echo my own.

I think for a moment before answering, "Well, a lot of the stuff is easy to learn, like putting out feed and water for the cattle. You could easily pick that up. Then, you could help me with the books, paying bills and stuff. Are you any good with numbers?"

"It wasn't my favorite subject in school. I know how to use a calculator though."

"It's basic stuff really. I'm sure you'd be fine. You could organize my office. My filing system is more like stacks of papers from the past couple of years. It needs attention pretty badly. It's just not high on my list of things to do, you know? Your hours could vary; it doesn't have to be full-time. Then, you'd have plenty of time to work up in your studio." As I talk everything out, Leni working for me makes more sense. Plus, I can't say that I don't love the fact that I'd see her every day.

She doesn't say anything for a beat. "Well, I suppose I could ... even if just for a while until I figure something else out. I could set you up with a sweet office space. That could be fun. The rest I can learn."

"Great. Plus, you can't beat the commute."

She laughs. "No, I definitely can't! Okay ... sounds like a plan."

Thirteen

Leni

A gust of wind pulls the fabric of my tad-too-short sundress off of my ass, and I can only hope that the goods remain covered. I told Mimi that it wasn't long enough, but she assured me that it was the perfect length. If I had known my hands would be completely occupied and unable to access the dress-over-my-ass situation, I'd have insisted that Mimi make it longer.

I feel completely out of place as I make my way across the lawn toward the backyard of Emily and Westley's home. First, I'm wearing pink and not just any pink; it's obnoxious bubblegum pink. Mimi says it's the perfect shade, but it reminds me of the gum that holds flavor for about two seconds but lets me blow huge bubbles.

The directions on the invitation were clear—*wear pink if you think it's going to be a girl, or wear blue if your guess is a boy.* And bring a dish to pass. That is why, in addition to my gift, I'm holding a heavy ceramic dish of baked beans, which, along with the dress, is also courtesy of Mimi.

I've never been to a gender-reveal party or any of the gatherings leading up to a baby—engagement parties, bridal showers, none of it. My peers in Elkwood seem to be about ten years ahead of the crowd I hung with in the city.

"Do you need help?" a familiar voice asks from behind me, amusement evident in his tone.

"Yes, please," I tell Liam, turning to give him the baked beans. "Where's your gift and dish to pass?" I shake out my cramped hand in front of me, admiring Liam.

He's in jeans and a blue flannel-printed button-up shirt.

"Dropped off the keg this morning, and the gift card is in my back pocket."

"Oh, that's smart. I should've just done a gift card."

"Well, I'm sure your gift is more thoughtful. What'd you get them anyway?" He eyes the large gift I'm holding.

I shrug. "Honestly, I have no idea. Mimi bought and wrapped it."

Liam throws his head back and laughs. "Oh, Leni."

"Hey, I'm trying. I'm wearing a new pink sundress. I mean, come on. You do realize that ninety percent of my limited wardrobe is black."

"Good job. You look great. The cowboy boots are a nice touch."

I grin. "Thanks. I thought so." I eye the smaller box on top of the large one in my arms. "And I lied. I do know what the small box is. I painted them a little canvas for the nursery," I admit.

"Ah, there she is." Liam chuckles.

"Who?" I question.

"The warmhearted version of yourself that you like to hide." He grins.

"Whatever. I'm not always cold."

"Not always. So, what did you paint them?"

"It's a cute little baby elephant. I even brought a brush and tube of blue and pink paint, so I can give it the appropriate-colored bow once we find out what the gender is."

"Look at you ... being all thoughtful."

I shrug. "I told you, I have my moments."

"I know you do," Liam says as we round toward the back of the house. His full and husky voice all of a sudden causes something in my belly to clench.

The backyard is full of people, most of whom seem familiar. I obviously didn't go to school here, but I think I've met a lot of these people through Liam or Emily at some point. It's set up exactly how I figured Emily's backyard party would be. There's a long table with food, another full of presents, and pink and blue balloons everywhere. Most of the guys are congregating around the grill with a Solo cup of beer in hand.

I set the presents down on the gift table.

"Leni!" Emily's cheerful voice calls my name before she pulls me into a hug. "I'm so glad you could make it." She holds me at arm's length and scans my attire. "So, you think it's going to be a girl, too?"

Her smile is so wide that I can't break it to her that Mimi had this fabric folded up in a cedar chest in one of the spare bedrooms, which was the only contributing factor to my color choice. "I sure do."

"I do, too." She shoots me a wink. "Of course, I'll be happy with either. But I just have a feeling. You know?"

No, I don't know at all, but I nod anyway.

Emily takes my hand. "Let me introduce you to everyone."

I stand around with a group of women all wearing varying shades of pink. Everyone is really nice. They all know and love Mimi, so that helps with the initial connection.

"So, Leni," Emily's friend Greta addresses me, "how is living in New York? Did you really like it? People say they love New York, but the only memories that stuck with me from when I was there as a child were all of the people everywhere and my dad screaming in rage at the other cars as we drove our rental through the city."

I chuckle. "Yeah, those are two of the downfalls of living there—the tourists and the traffic. But I can honestly say that I did love it. You get used to all the people, and after a while, you find a cadence to the madness, you know? When I first got here, I missed the hustle and bustle of the city. And I never drove there. I truly don't know how people do. I'm all about the public transportation. Less stress for sure. Your dad is a trooper for navigating through that traffic."

"Well, I'm pretty sure it took ten years off of his life," Greta kids.

"Are you going to go back?" another friend asks me.

"I'm not sure. I'm open to move anywhere that my art will sell."

"What kind of art do you do again?" Emily asks.

"A little bit of everything, though painting is my favorite."

"Well, I hope you don't move away anytime soon. Mrs. Turner will be heartbroken. She loves having you here," Emily says.

I smile warmly. "I know she does. I love being here with her, too."

I get asked a few more questions about New York, and I listen as the girls gossip about other stuff. This whole thing is strange—for me anyway—but oddly nice. Perhaps this is what it would've been like in high school had I tried to make friends. But I was content with being a sullen loner. I think I held so much resentment in my heart, growing up, that not only did I close out my parents, but almost everyone else as well. For the first time in my life, I kind of feel bad about it.

I look across the yard to see Liam staring at me. When my eyes lock with his, his lips turn up into a sexy grin, and I smirk before smiling back. I can admit that I'm glad we're friends again. As weird as this all is, it's nice, too—being social, wearing pink, laughing with a group of giggling women, having Liam back. I don't hate it.

My smile fades when Camila shows up next to Liam and wraps her arms around him. He hugs her back. I pull my stare from Liam and turn my attention back to Emily and her friends. They're all talking and laughing about something, but I don't hear a word they're saying. My stomach aches as my body is overcome with intense nausea.

This is stupid.

I excuse myself and head inside to use the bathroom. I'm shocked at the visceral reaction I felt when seeing Liam with Camila. It's ridiculous. We're barely friends, let alone anything else. I shouldn't care what he does or who he does it with.

What is wrong with me? I'm a nutcase.

I finish washing my hands and stare into the bathroom mirror, taking deep, steadying breaths. I don't want to go back out there. In fact, everything in me wants to just skip out of the front door and give my apologies to Emily later. But that wouldn't be cool. I actually like this pink-wearing, semi-social, bread-eating, smiling person I've been as of late. I'm not going to let my emotions get the best of me.

The greatest detriment to my happiness has been me for as long as I can remember and all in the name of self-preservation. I'm not the girl trapped in her parents' house of evil anymore. There's no cause to run. Liam isn't mine, nor do I want him to be. I'll be leaving here soon anyway.

I have no reason to feel weird about my friend dating someone regardless of who he chooses to date. Camila would probably be my last choice for him, but it's his life. My head knows what's right; my brain is capable of rationalizing it all. But my heart and body aren't following suit.

"Just stop," I whisper toward the mirror. "Be normal," I chastise with a squint of my eyes, causing me to grin at my own ridiculousness.

Letting out a sigh, I step back from the sink and open the bathroom door to rejoin the party.

My eyes go wide, and my step falters. Liam is leaning against the wall with one leg bent, his cowboy boot positioned against the hard surface, propping him up. His arms are crossed over his chest. He pushes off of the wall with his boot and turns so that we're face-to-face.

"Are you okay? I saw you go into the house. You didn't look well."

He wears a look of concern, and it kind of pisses me off. I'm not his problem.

"I'm fine." I step to his side, eager to distance myself from him.

"Len"—he grabs my arm—"what is it? I can tell something's wrong."

He sounds sincere, and knowing Liam, he probably is, but it annoys me just the same.

"Just stop, Liam. I'm not your problem. I'm a big girl, and I can handle myself." I shake my arm from his grasp. "Just go hang out with your girlfriend. I'm fine, really." I press my lips into a tight smile and give him a reassuring nod before heading back out.

In the backyard, Emily and Westley are standing under a tall tree with a giant gray balloon hanging from the lowest outstretched branch.

I join the semicircle of guests around them, waiting for the big reveal.

Liam positions himself beside me. "I don't have a girlfriend," his gravelly voice whispers into my ear, making my skin break into violent goose bumps.

I swallow hard. "I don't care one way or the other."

His fingers glide over the needy bumps present on my arm. "Are you sure about that?" he asks.

I bite my lower lip and nod, words escaping me.

"Okay, well, I'm not involved with anyone, but that doesn't mean that there's not someone I'm interested in. If you ever want to talk about that, you just let me know."

As he pulls his mouth away, he raises his hand and tucks a lock of my hair behind my ear. The simple motion, seemingly innocent, weighs heavy on my emotions. I lock my knees to stop them from buckling.

Voices ring out around us, counting down from ten. As Liam joins in the countdown, he drops his arm to the side. The top of his hand skims against my skin, and he hooks his pinkie finger with mine.

Emily pops the balloon. Cheers erupt as pink confetti showers down around her and Westley.

I can't remember the last time I smiled so wide, the effects of which I can feel all the way down to my toes.

fourteen

Leni

Liam wasn't lying when he said his office could use some work. When he first offered me the job, I thought it was just to be nice—a favor to me. And, though I think it started that way, now that I'm here, I realize he needs some help. He's so busy all the time with things that have to be done on the ranch that he doesn't have time for the things that should be done in his office.

I'm sitting on the office floor, legs crossed, amid piles of paperwork when Liam walks in, carrying two brown bags.

"I brought lunch, courtesy of Mimi," he says with a smile. "Wanna head outside for a picnic?"

I shake my head. "I can't." I continue when I see his smile fade, "I can't lose my place, Liam. Look." I point to a stack of receipts next to me. "These are the expenses from the first quarter of the year. Then, these are the second." I place my finger atop another pile. I continue to point to all the piles around me. "This is the third quarter. These are expenses and itemized deductions. These are your mile calculations. These are the receipts that have been added up, and these still need to be." After I've explained what another twenty piles are, I say, "I can't get up now. I know this doesn't look organized, but as long as I sit right here, I know what everything is. If I get up and lose my bearings, I'm going to be so lost. I can't go through all these papers again." I move my head from side to side. "I wouldn't make it," I say dramatically with a laugh.

Liam chuckles. "Okay, but as long as you stay in that position … you're good?"

"Yes." I nod. "As long as I sit right here, I know what everything is, and it all makes sense. It's organized chaos. If I move at this point, it's going to be just utter chaos."

"All right. Well then, we'll have a picnic right here on the floor. Sound good?"

"Yes!"

"So, I'm just going to plop down right here in front of …" He points to a stack of receipts.

"Those are the ones I have questions about," I answer.

"Perfect," he says. "Well, we can address those after lunch."

He hands me a sacked lunch, and I pull out a sandwich.

"Thank you. I'm starving. So, how's life out on the ranch today?"

"Good. You should come out when you're able to leave your insane amount of piles. There are several cows that are due to give birth any day. You might catch a birth."

"Really?" I ask in awe.

"Yeah. Remember the first time you saw one?"

"I do." I nod. "What were we? Seven and eight?"

"Yeah, it was your second summer here, so you were seven."

I think back to that early summer day. Liam excitedly ran up to Mimi's and grabbed me by the hand, telling me that a cow was having a baby. The two of us sprinted as fast as we could across Mimi's land until we made it to the cow. I remember the birth itself being a little gross but fascinating. The baby calf was the cutest thing ever though.

"Oh, I love how the calves suck your fingers. Remember that?"

I recall going to visit that fuzzy little calf every day. He would suck on my pointer finger like it was a bottle. Liam and I used to giggle nonstop when we put our fingers in the calf's mouth.

Liam wears a wistful smile. "Yeah, I do."

"Do you remember what we named the first one I saw being born? It was something with an R."

"You named him Rusty Roo." Liam grins.

"Oh, that's right." I nod. "I get the Rusty part because of his coloring, but where did I get the Roo part?"

"I have no idea." He chuckles, shaking his head.

"That was a fun summer."

"It was," Liam agrees. "Do you remember what else you did that summer the day before your mom came to get you?"

I let out a sigh. "Uh, yeah. I took Mimi's kitchen shears, pulled my hair back in a ponytail, and cut it right off. I knew my mother would hate my hair short. I was a rebellious little thing, wasn't I?"

"Was? As in past tense?" he kids.

"Ha-ha." I squint my eyes toward Liam. "You would have been, too, if you'd had a mother like mine."

"Probably so."

"Oh, definitely so. Your mom is nice and normal. Mine is just so ..." My voice trails off because I can't think of the right words to describe my mother.

Distant? Cold? Snobby? Cruel?

Maybe cruel is a little harsh. She never physically hurt me, but I've come to realize that words are often more damaging than physical marks, even the ones left unsaid. She never stood up for me once against my father. Maybe it would have been better if she'd hit me. Maybe then she wouldn't have felt the need to lash out at me with her vile statements so often. Over time, the memories of her words have faded. But then there are some exchanges between the two of us that will forever be ingrained in my mind, weighing deeply on my heart. No matter how often I tell myself that it doesn't matter what my parents think of me or say to me, there's a small girl within me who still aches for the approval that will never come.

"Hey"—Liam gently touches the top of my hand— "where'd you go?"

I press my lips together in a line before saying, "It doesn't matter."

"It does though."

"Nah, I don't really want to talk about my parents, Liam. You and I both know the type of people they are. There's no use in wasting a second of my time worrying over what I wish they'd do or say or what they hadn't done or said. It's not important."

"Well, sometimes, it helps to talk about it. Maybe, if you give voice to your pain, you can let it go." He sets his bottle of water down and extends his arms out toward me, taking my hands in his.

134

I suck in a breath at his touch. His grasp is so firm yet comforting. His skin is rough yet soothing. I look from our joined hands up to his face. I swallow and clear my throat.

"I don't want to talk about it," I say again, more softly this time.

"All right. Well, if you do, you know I'm here for you. I'm a good listener." Liam gives me a warm smile.

I still don't understand why he cares so much for me, given our history, but I'm grateful that he does.

"Okay," I almost whisper.

My gaze falls back down to our hands, which are still entwined together. My heart pounds rapidly within my chest as I wait for Liam to let me go. I bring my stare up to meet his.

His grasp remains steady. With just this simple gesture, he makes me feel accepted, content, and though it causes the butterflies to take flight within my belly, I feel *cherished*.

My eyes find his, and I'm lost. My heartbeats become louder within me, each one pumping out a rhythm, a frenzied beat of palpitations that are partially confused and needy.

His penetrating stare holds me in this place where time is measured by weighted breaths and a nervous swallow, the thumping of my heart and a bite of my lip. I should pull my hand from his. I should break our gaze, but I can't, and sweet baby Jesus … I don't want to. He lowers his eyes to my lips before his rub together.

I see the intent in his eyes as he leans in. I hesitate only a moment before I move forward to meet him.

The small voice in my head tells me to stop, but I can't. I won't.

He releases my hands and raises his. The skin of his palm lightly grazes my cheek before he threads his fingers through my hair. He tightens his grip against my scalp and pulls slightly before his lips find mine. I release a groan into his mouth, unable to stop it.

His lips are soft and incredibly intoxicating as they move against my own. I raise my hands to his face and cover his cheeks and strong jaw. My body trembles with what feels like years of want for Liam Moore.

Soft kisses become harder. My mouth opens wider, allowing Liam's tongue to enter, moving with mine in a dance that only we could make. The kiss is unlike anything I've ever experienced. It's real. It's raw. And it's perfect. Though I've kissed before, Liam's mouth makes me realize that I've never truly been kissed, never like this.

I never want it to stop. In fact, I want so much more. Liam seems to read my mind because he lowers us to the ground, his lips never leaving mine. Papers crinkle beneath my back as Liam's strong body presses against me. I run my hands down his face and grip his arms. He's so strong, and his perfectly sculpted muscles are so incredible; I want to drag my tongue over every single one.

Liam keeps one hand threaded in my hair and continues to pull my face into his while his free hand trails over my body. My skin burns beneath his touch, and I want more. I want him to rip my clothes off and touch me everywhere. The need between my legs is almost unbearable, and I want to beg Liam to touch me there, but he doesn't.

We've been kissing for so long that I can barely feel my lips when he pulls away. I gasp as I pull air into my lungs. My entire body hums with desire. Liam lies beside me as we stare toward the ceiling.

Wow, is all I can think.

Liam Moore has skills. I'm honestly not surprised. I somehow always knew he did.

I'm the first to speak. "That was ..." I'm unable to put my reaction to the kiss into words.

"Yeah," Liam agrees. He turns to the side and faces me, resting his head on his propped up hand. "I think some of your piles got ruined."

I pout my lips before the corners rise into a grin. "It seems they did." I dismissively wave my hand before me. "Whatever. You're the one paying me to organize them all again."

"And it's completely worth it." Liam tucks a lock of my hair behind my ear. "I have a secret to tell you."

I turn toward him and rest my head up on my hand, mirroring him. "What's that?"

Our faces are mere inches apart, and my recently slowed heart starts to increase its cadence once more.

Liam brings his thumb up to my lips and pulls them down. He breathes in deeply. "I've loved you for as long as I can remember, Leni Turner."

My eyes go wide, and my lungs seem to stop working because I suddenly can't breathe. Every feeling that I experienced growing up floods my sensations now. Fear. Despair. Heartache. Disappointment. I remember what it was like to live through them all. My dad's cruelty weighs heavily on me, and my mom's entrapment tightens my throat with panic. I can't breathe.

Somewhere deep within my heart, I know Liam isn't my dad, and I'm not my mom. But I haven't accomplished anything that I want to. I can't fall for Liam, and the fact is that he's easy to fall for, to love. I've seen what love does to one's dreams, one's life; I've lived it. I've worked too hard my entire life to escape this place. I can't afford to be weak now.

I jump up from the floor and press my fingers to my temples.

Crap. Crap. Crap.

"Don't freak out. It's not a big deal. I just felt like telling you that after that kiss. I didn't mean to scare you"—he gestures toward me—"or make you feel however it is that you're feeling right now. Breathe, Leni. Your face is turning red."

I suck in air and hold my hand out when Liam tries to come closer to comfort me.

"Liam," I say sadly with a shake of my head.

Ugh. I should've known. With a kiss like that, of course he has feelings for me. I'm so stupid.

"Len, it doesn't change anything. We can still continue as we are. We can take it slow."

I release a sigh. Frowning, I look into his worried brown eyes. "It changes everything, Liam. We can't … I mean, I … it's not like that for me. You're not right for me. This place isn't right for me. I'm getting out of Texas the second I can. This isn't where I'm supposed to be."

I search his eyes, praying to find understanding. He has to know that something between us could never work.

"I'm sorry. I shouldn't have kissed you," I say. "It was a mistake."

"It sure as hell didn't feel like a mistake, Leni. I know you felt it, too. There's something really good here."

He reaches out for me, and I take a step back.

"Do you know what I felt, Liam? I felt horny. Nothing more. I can't love you. I can't be with you the way that you want me to. It's never been in the cards for me, and you know it." My voice quivers with anger—toward me, with Liam, over this whole situation.

Truthfully, I can only be mad at myself. Regardless of whether or not I acknowledged it, I saw the emotions within Liam building. The sweetness, the grand gestures, the flirty smiles, the way he always seems to be watching me. I knew; of course I knew. And yet I let the situation get out of control. I let him freaking kiss me. Yeah, this is all on me.

Liam stares at me, his expression pained.

"I ... I'm going to call it a day. I'll work on this mess tomorrow."

He nods once, and I walk out of the office as quickly as possible. I don't turn back around to look at him before I leave, but I don't need to. I know the heartbreaking expression he wears without even seeing it. I know it because I saw it when I was sixteen, and it's been haunting me ever since.

fifteen

Liam
Age Seventeen

This is a mistake. I walk toward Mrs. Turner's house. *This is a huge mistake.*

I'm trying to wrap my brain around everything I felt when I saw Leni last night at Westley's party. She was every bit the girl I'd met in the cornfields so many years ago, but at the same time, she was nothing like her. She made it clear during our brief conversation in the barn that nothing had changed from last year. Our lack of friendship is still the status quo, and yet I find myself walking up to her grandma's front porch. I can't stay away. I've never been able to.

Leni hasn't been a real friend for a few years now. Everything changed the summer of my fourteenth birthday, and I'm not entirely sure why. She says that our friendship isn't good for her, but it doesn't make sense. I know the kind of life that she lives during the school year, and it isn't a pleasant one. She used to always tell me that spending her summers with me and Mrs. Turner was the only thing that saved her the other nine months. So, what's changed?

I pause in front of the old wooden door to the farmhouse. My inner voice tells me to leave, and I know I should listen. This isn't going to end the way I want it to, but I can't make my feet lead me away.

I love Leni. I've loved her from the moment I met her, our connection instant. At six years old with mud covering my skin and a toothless grin, I knew that I wanted to be around her as much as possible. Our friendship was destined, our souls fated. When we were together, we were seamlessly happy—until we weren't.

So, I have to try—one more time. I have to try for the Leni I love, not for the purple-haired sprite that excels at breaking me with her words. I know that my best friend is under all of that anger that she holds at the surface, and I know she needs me.

I lift my fist to the door, and I knock.

A space that feels like an eternity passes until the door opens. She stands in front of me. A bandana is wrapped around her head, hiding her violet chunks. She's wearing jean shorts, a tank top, and not an ounce of makeup. Her stunning greens capture my browns, and I'm frozen in this period of hope before any cutting words have been spoken. In these few seconds, I find it hard to breathe, longing for the outcome I need.

I clear my throat, willing my words to come. "Hey."

She steps out into the scorching summer heat, closing the door behind her. "Hi," she answers.

"I know last night was … weird. I don't know. I just thought maybe we could hang out," I ramble.

"I don't know." She shakes her head, her gaze focused toward the ground.

"Do you want to drive into town or something? We could get some ice cream," I offer. "Please."

She raises her stare to meet mine, and we stay locked in uncertainty until she finally releases a sigh.

"Okay, let me go tell Mimi."

I wait anxiously for a couple of minutes for her to return. She does, and we start walking toward the truck.

"Did you have a good time last night?" I ask.

"Not particularly." She shrugs.

"Well ..." I start to reply, but realizing I have nothing to say, I close my mouth.

We get into the truck, and silence surrounds us as I pull out of Mimi's driveway.

I head toward town and notice Leni picking at her nails. There are remnants of black nail polish still there.

I nod toward her hands. "Black, huh?"

"Yeah. I attempted to anger my mom by becoming goth this past year," she says.

"Goth?"

"Yep."

"How goth? Are we talking black clothes and lots of dark makeup?"

I can't imagine Leni with that style, but I'm sure she wore it well. She wears everything well.

"Oh, yeah. As dark as I could be. You know, all black clothes, black leather bands around my wrists and neck, black nails, combat boots, and eyeliner and dark makeup for days."

"I'm sure it drove your parents insane." I laugh.

"Pretty much. My mom's been angry for a year straight. I'm surprised she hasn't given herself a stroke or something. Dad's been busy. I don't see him much anyway, and when I do, he just looks at me with an indifferent expression. I think he's over caring, not that he ever cared anyway."

"Well, I'm so glad you're here. As I told you last night, I think the purple looks good."

Leni scoffs but doesn't reply.

"Listen, Len, I know what you said last night, but I just don't get it. I don't understand the animosity between us. Truthfully, it doesn't matter. It's just so good to see you. I've missed you like crazy." I open up to her despite my better judgment. Yet the only way I know how to be with Leni is honest.

She was my confidant for so long; it's impossible for me to hide my feelings from her, and I don't want to. I want our friendship back. I want my Leni back. The one who had a way of making every summer break nothing short of magical. The one who would talk my ear off. The one who would make me laugh until I had tears streaming down my face. My best friend. My Leni girl.

Leni steals a look in my direction, and I see the longing in her eyes. She misses me, too. Her wistful expression is present for only a second before it falls, leaving a grimace in its wake. The atmosphere within the truck cab changes instantly.

"Take me back," Leni demands, her voice cold and firm.

"Leni," I reply soothingly.

"Now, William! Take me back."

After a quick look in my mirrors, I brake and turn the steering wheel, doing a U-turn in the road. Leni holds on to the dash as the tires squeal against the pavement.

I squeeze the steering wheel until my hands hurt. I've never been an angry person, but Leni makes me so furious that I just want to punch something. I only have a few minutes with her before we're back at her grandma's farm, and I have a sick feeling that these few fleeting moments are the last I'll have with her this summer. We're right back to where we were last year, and I'm just as confused.

"What in the hell is wrong? I don't get it," I yell.

Leni clamps her lips closed and looks out the window, set on ignoring me.

"No, I want answers. This isn't fair," I huff out.

"Life isn't fair, William. Get over it."

"I deserve to know why our friendship has resorted to this. Damn it, Leni. I haven't done anything wrong, yet you treat me like shit. I want to know why." My grasp on the steering wheel is so tight that my hands have started to go numb. I spread out my fingers on each hand, allowing the blood to flow again.

We pull into her grandma's drive, and she reaches for the door handle.

I grab her hand. "Stop. Before you go stomping away, I want to know what's going on. I deserve to know."

My stare catches hers and holds her there. I see the pain and regret in her eyes, but those feelings don't translate to her words.

"We're not friends. We haven't been for a long time. There's nothing to say, except that you need to get over it."

"Leni—" I begin.

"No! You're not listening to me. I don't want any sort of relationship with you. I can't. Why won't you accept that?" Her shrill voice shakes.

"It doesn't add up," I tell her.

She shrugs. "It doesn't matter. It has to be this way. Let it go. Let me go. You have your friends. You have

Bella. You don't need me. Stop forcing something that isn't there."

"Is this about Bella? She and I aren't—"

Leni cuts me off, "This isn't about Bella or anyone else you make out with. This is about me and what I need. You're not good for me, Liam. I can't." She shakes her head, and remorse covers her face.

Her eyes well with unshed tears, and I want to pull her into a hug, but I don't.

I shake my head. "I can't keep trying," I softly tell her.

"Then, don't," she whispers.

Her words, full of conviction, slice me open, leaving a gash so deep that I know it will never fully heal. There are so many things I want to say, but the words don't come. I know, in this moment, that this is it. This will be my last few seconds with Leni.

I know we're meant to be friends. I see it in her eyes, just as I feel it in my heart. I want to tell her again that she's wrong. I want to beg her to reason. I want to do and say so many things, but I can't.

I'm done.

I've tried so many times. I've ignored her words, listening only to my heart, but as much as I want Leni in my life, I can't force her to want me.

All I can do is watch as she jumps down from the truck and slams the door. My heart breaks as she walks off toward the house. I pray for a backward glance, any indication that she regrets the last few moments, but none comes. She walks away from me with purpose.

Right now, there's an eerie vacancy within my chest, a hole that I'd give anything to fill. I know that it will never again be filled with Leni. And it just fucking sucks.

Sixteen

Leni
Age Sixteen

As soon as Mimi's front door closes behind me, the tears start to fall, hard and fast. I choke on air as I pull it into my lungs. I replay everything I just said to Liam, and I feel nauseous. I'm a dreadful person. Truly, I am.

I'm selfish and cruel. I know my words hurt him so deeply that he won't be back, probably ever. It was intentional, too. I hate this version of myself, the one who pushes away my only real friend. Truthfully, I hate every aspect of my life—except Mimi. I could never hate Mimi. Yet everything else is utter shit.

I just have to make it two more years, and then I can leave Texas forever and never come back. I'm so sad and alone. My chest aches all the time with excruciating pain that never leaves me. I don't know who I am anymore or who I'm meant to be. I do recognize the unhappiness that follows me everywhere I go. I'm certain the answers I need aren't here. Self-discovery isn't going to be found in the stuffy walls of my parents' home or in the comfy walls of Mimi's. They're not going to be found in Texas.

I'm not sure who I am, but I'm certain, with crystal-clear clarity, who I'm not. I'm not my mother. I'm not a rich and proper debutante. I'm not someone who is going to sacrifice all her happiness for someone else. I'm not someone who is going to fall in love with Liam and be trapped here forever. As much as my heart wants to love him, my mind and will are much stronger.

It's impossible to be around Liam and not fall for him. He's perfect for me in every way. He knows me better than anyone else. He's the only person in the world who gets me. And that's why we can't be friends. When I became a teenager and the hormones kicked in, everything changed. The second I saw Liam differently, the second I felt my stomach do excited flips at his presence, the very second I saw his lips as something I wanted, I knew that I couldn't have him in my life.

Liam Moore isn't someone I can casually be friends with. He isn't someone I can have a fling with. Liam is someone I would love forever. He's someone who would make me want to stay, and that's why he's more dangerous than anything my parents could throw my way. He's the person who could keep me here, in this life that's killing me. I would love him as I faded, but I'd fade away just the same.

seventeen

Leni

I lie, sprawled out on the couch, a plate of deliciousness in my lap. "Mimi, you're an enabler," I say through a mouthful of freshly baked bread and jam.

Mimi chuckles from her rocking chair, holding a mug of tea.

"Seriously, stop making me feel better for being a horrible human being." I take another bite of bread. A glob of butter falls onto my shirt. "Crap." I sit up, bring my shirt to my mouth, and lick it off.

"You should go put that in the washer. Butter will leave a grease stain," Mimi tells me.

"Good. It's what I deserve. You know what? You're right; I'm my own worst enemy. I don't know why I do what I do. I'm mean. I push people away. Why do I do that?" I beg Mimi for answers.

"Are you ready to tell me what happened?" Mimi asks, her voice soothing.

"He kissed me." I shrug. "Then, he told me that he's always loved me, so I said something that I knew would hurt his feelings, and then I walked away. Why do I do that? Why do I say things to hurt him when he's always been so nice to me? It's just like when I was sixteen." I shake my head, thinking back to the cruel words I said to him then.

"Did you want him to kiss you?" she asks.

"Yes," I admit. "But I don't want him to love me."

She scoffs. "Well, my dear, sometimes, you don't have control over that. What's wrong with him loving you? You're worthy of love."

"No, I'm not. Not his. I'm going to hurt him and leave him. He doesn't deserve that—again."

"Why do you say that? How do you know you'll do those things?"

I sigh. "Because it's what I do, Mimi. I alienate myself from people. I'm not going to stay here. I can't live in Texas! What if I fall for him, and then I'm stuck here forever? I will have ruined my life. I'm an artist. I'm not meant to be here. I have to stay focused on my goals, my dreams. I can't settle. I won't change who I am for love. And you know what? Liam is the type of guy who will make me want to. So, why would I allow something to happen when I know how it will end? I'm trying to be the good guy here, but I know he only sees me as the bad one."

"Let me tell you a story," Mimi says. "Once, there was a little princess whose energy was so bright that it lit up the room when she entered. She was smart and funny. She was artistic and brave. She loved with her whole heart, and she wore her emotions on her sleeve. This sweet girl lived with her parents, the king and queen. Her parents possessed none of the same qualities. They were cold and selfish. They valued things like power and money over family and happiness. They tried to change the free-spirited princess. But she refused to let them dull her sparkle. Yet, over time, the king and queen pushed the princess down so much that she had a hard time getting up. But she did ... time and time again. Yet, each time she rose from the insults, she would put another layer of protection over her heart, and in doing so, she started to drive away the ones who loved her."

Mimi stops to take a sip of her tea. Unwanted tears fall from my eyes, and my lip trembles.

Mimi continues, "She vowed to herself that she would never be like her parents. She set goals for her life, and the second she could break free, she did. Except, now, she kept her bright energy buried. She guarded her heart and withheld her love. Because, though the princess was strong, she was scared. She'd been let down by those who were supposed to love her the most. She didn't realize it, but she was pushing away those who could love her in the future, out of fear of the past and getting hurt again.

"But what the princess needs to understand is that people like her parents are not the norm, and by guarding her heart, she's forever condemning herself to a life of loneliness. Sure, she might get hurt in the future, but if she doesn't try, she'll never be set free. She'll never be truly happy."

Mimi sets her tea down on the end table beside her and rises from her rocker. She comes over to me and sits beside me, wrapping her loving arms around my shoulders. I lean into her and cry.

"I don't want to be stuck here," I say with a sniffle.

"Leni girl, Texas isn't the enemy. A place doesn't make or break your happiness; the people you surround yourself with do. You're already an artist regardless of where you call home. I know you're trying to get away from everything associated with your parents, but, honey, you're only hurting yourself."

"I'm really messed up, aren't I?"

"No, you're not. You've created a life you thought you needed to in order to distance yourself from your parents, but, my girl, you're nothing like them." Mimi sadly shakes her head. "I wish I could've done more. Know that I tried. I begged to keep you full-time, but they wouldn't have it. I was lucky to get you for the summers."

"The only reason you got summers was probably because they were so annoyed with me. I didn't make it easy on them throughout the school year." I can't help but smile.

"You were and are a tenacious little thing." She wipes some of my tear-soaked hair off my face. "I admire that about you. So much." Mimi looks me in the eyes. "Leni, you are no longer a little girl without options. You're a grown woman. Your parents no longer have any control over you. So, stop giving it to them. Make your own decisions. Be the person you're meant to be. Live a good life."

"So, you think I should give Liam a chance?" I ask.

"I think you should listen to your heart. Don't let fear control your decisions, but instead, let hope guide them. I don't know if Liam is the one for you, sweetie, and you won't either unless you try. I do know that boy has a heart of gold, and he has adored you since the two of you were young. He's something special, and whether it's you or someone else … he's going to make some lady really happy someday." She smiles warmly.

"Yeah, he's definitely one of the good ones," I agree. "He's really nothing like my father, is he?"

Mimi actually snorts, and it causes me to laugh along with her. "Absolutely not! Is that what you're worried about? That you'll end up with someone like your dad?"

I nod my head because, deep down, I think that's my biggest fear. I saw what love for my father turned my mother into, and I vowed early on that I would never love someone the way my mother loved my father. I would never lose myself like that.

"Leni, you grew up with a horrible example of what love is. I wish you had been older when your pops passed. He was a good man, and we loved each other as much as two people could. It was beautiful. I want that for you." She grins at me before pulling me into a hug.

I hug her tight because I don't know where I'd be today without her. I only got her in the summers, but it was enough to keep me sane. It was enough to keep me fighting.

"I love you so much," I tell her. I realize I probably don't tell her that enough.

"And I love you more than anything, my Leni girl. You're going to be okay."

I take off my butter-stained shirt and wash my face. After running a brush through my hair, I throw it up into a ponytail.

I have to go find Liam and apologize. I've hurt him too much in the past. It's time to grow the hell up and make it right. The talk with Mimi just now really resonated with me. She's totally right; I'm an adult. I get to choose how I'm going to live my life, and there's no way I'm going to let my parents' darkness control my decisions anymore.

I find Liam out in the barn, fussing over a baby calf.

"Oh my goodness. She's so adorable," I say, causing Liam to turn around.

He smiles weakly. "She sure is," he says before turning away.

"Um, listen, Liam ... I was wondering if I could talk to you." I don't miss the way his back rises and falls in response to my words.

He wipes his hands on his jeans. "Leni, it's fine. You made yourself clear. It won't happen again. Let's move on. I can't do this with you again."

I know he's referring to everything I put him through when we were teenagers. Guilt fills my chest.

I pull in a deep breath, and I continue, "I want to tell you that I'm sorry. I'm so sorry ... for everything. I had no right to treat you as my punching bag when we were younger. I had no right to say what I did back in the office."

He turns to face me and scoffs, "Well, at least you're honest. Right?"

"But that's the thing. I'm not, and I haven't been honest with you or anyone else for a long time. I've just been ... lost, I guess. I truly don't want what I said in your office. I said it to push you away." I chuckle dryly. "I suppose I've said a lot of things over the years to push you away."

He pins me with his stare, and in it, I see hope.

"What are you saying, Len?"

I let out a loud breath. "I'm saying, I'm sorry."

"And?" he questions.

"I didn't mean any of the words I said to you—earlier in your office or in the past."

"So, you didn't kiss me just because you were horny?"

He raises an eyebrow, and, damn it, even when he smirks, he's sexy.

"Ugh," I groan, my cheeks heating with embarrassment. "No, that wasn't why. I'm sorry."

"I accept your apology, and thank you. It means a lot." He smiles, the sadness from just moments ago absent from his gaze. "So, friends?"

I shake my head. "I don't think I want that," I say softly.

He exhales and lets his head fall back. He looks up toward the ceiling, his body rigid.

"Or I guess I should say that I don't think I want *just* that."

He lowers his head and squints in question.

I step toward him, closing the space between us. "Of course I want to be friends. Despite everything, you're the truest friend I've ever had. But you were right back there. I did feel it. That kiss was the most beautiful kiss I've ever had. It made me feel things that I didn't know I could."

He steps in closer, putting his hands around my waist. His fingers press into my skin, causing all sorts of emotions to course through me.

"And?" he questions, lowering his face until it's a whisper away from mine.

I swallow. "And I want to do it again."

I don't have to ask twice. The second the words leave my mouth, Liam's hands cradle my face as his lips press against mine. The kiss is everything that it was before, except, now, it's even more incredible somehow. This time, I asked for it, and I finally realize how much I truly want Liam, how I've always wanted him.

Liam picks me up, and I wrap my legs around his waist. He pushes my back up against the coarse wooden wall of the barn as his lips continue their unbelievable assault.

As our kiss continues, I allow my guard to fall, releasing all the pent-up rage that's been simmering beneath the surface for so long.

I just feel.

I take Liam in—his scent, his sounds, and the way his tongue continues to caress my own, as if kissing me is its sole purpose. Most importantly, I stop denying my heart, and I let it fill up with everything that is Liam. For the first time, I allow it to love who it wants, who it's always wanted.

My body shakes with desire. Liam's kisses leave my mouth and continue their mind-blowing worship against the skin of my neck. I vaguely register the sound of my moans into the open space, but they don't make me feel uncomfortable. If anything, the unrestrained noises of pleasure cause me to need Liam even more.

"I want you," I pant as Liam's hand moves up my chest and under my bra. "God, I want you. Please, Liam," I say on an exhale, moving my body in a rhythmic motion against his.

The pleasure is astonishing. I can't wait to get our clothes off.

Liam stops kissing me and pulls his hand from beneath my shirt. He presses the palms of his hands against my cheeks. His warm exhale blows across my skin as he leans his forehead against mine.

"Leni." His voice is rough with need.

"Liam." His name leaves my lips with palpable want.

"We need to stop." His words bring me back to myself.

"What? Why? No." I shake my head.

I don't want to stop. I want to keep going and then go some more. I want Liam in every way I can get him, and I want him now.

He leans back and lightly kisses me where his forehead was just resting against mine. "I just got you. I'm not going to spook you and risk losing you."

"I won't get spooked," I protest, dropping my legs to the ground.

"I know," he agrees with a smirk. "Because we're not going to rush into anything that will scare you away."

"I promise," I almost whine. "Come on. I swear. I'll sign something." I feverishly look around, as if looking for a nonexistent contract. "Pinkie promise! Liam!" I say frantically.

He shakes his head with a grin and steps away from me. I follow him as he makes his way toward the stable with the newly born calf.

"Do you find this amusing?"

"A little."

"You're not playing fair. You can't kiss me like that and pull away like it has no effect on you."

"Leni, baby, everything about you turns me on. But I have lots of practice at pretending like it doesn't."

I cross my arms over my chest and throw my face into a dramatic pout. "I'm not very happy with you."

Liam pulls my face into a kiss. It's short and sweet, but it's everything.

"We're taking it slow," he tells me when he steps away. "Come help me with the calf."

We put new straw into the stall and get the new mama and her baby all set up for the night. I stick my index finger toward the cute little thing, and she starts to suck my finger. It tickles, and I giggle just like I did when

I was young. Liam laughs beside me. I pull my finger from the baby's mouth and wipe the dripping saliva that lingers on Liam's shirt.

"Nice. Thanks for that." He chuckles.

"You're welcome," I tease. "Do you want to have dinner with Mimi and me?"

"Sure. I'll wash up and change my clothes first."

"Can I name her?" I nod toward the calf.

"Yeah, of course … if you want. Do you have a name in mind?"

"I think I want to call her Hope," I answer.

Liam nods. "I like that. Hope it is."

I leave Liam in the barn to shower for dinner, and I head back up to the house. I stop in the yard and take in my surroundings. It really is so beautiful here. The chatter and chirps of the resident bugs and birds have started now that dusk is drawing near. The sky is colorful, and the air is warm against my skin.

It's hard to believe the gamut of emotions that I encountered just today, but they were all long overdue. I feel lighter.

Happier.

I'm not certain of the future Liam and I will have, but I'm really excited to find out. Hope has pushed out the fear in my heart, and I feel good.

Really.

Really.

Good.

eighteen

Liam

My foot hits Leni's from under the kitchen table. She looks up to me with a mouth full of mashed potatoes and grins as she taps my foot back.

"Everything is delicious, Mary," my dad says to Mrs. Turner.

"Yes, just wonderful," my mom says.

"Thank you. My pleasure." Mrs. Turner places butter on her roll, a content smile across her face.

"So, Leni, I just love the painting of this farm that you did for Liam. It's stunning. Would you be willing to do one of our farm? I'd love to hang it over the mantel," my mom says to Leni.

"Of course. I'd love to. Any excuse to paint," Leni answers.

"We would pay you, of course. Just let me know how much," my mom says.

"Oh, no." Leni waves her hand through the air. "No payment is necessary. It's good practice, and I love doing it."

These dinners with my parents at Mrs. Turner's house are becoming a regular thing, and it's great. Mrs. Turner loves cooking for others, and my parents love family dinners. My mom used to host Sunday dinner with all of my aunts and uncles, but many of them have moved away, and I know she misses it.

Unlike Leni's parents who only ever wanted one child, my mom wanted a whole house full of kids. Unfortunately, after I was born, my mom was diagnosed with ovarian cancer and had a hysterectomy shortly thereafter. She's never been one to complain, but I can see the joy in her face when she hosts our extended family. It's the same expression she's wearing now.

Leni takes a big bite of her dinner roll, and when she pulls the roll away, there's a dab of butter on her nose. I let out a quiet laugh and shake my head.

"What?" Leni questions.

I point to my nose, and Leni lifts her finger to hers, feeling the butter on her skin.

"Oops." She giggles and grabs her napkin.

"Saving it for later?" I smirk.

"Maybe I was. You never know when you'll need some butter." She narrows her eyes in my direction in mock annoyance.

"Very true."

After dinner, Leni and I do the dishes and clean up the kitchen before heading outside to the porch swing. There's a full moon casting a light glow over the ground tonight. The symphony of chirping frogs and the buzzing insects is noisier than usual. The boisterous cadence of the wildlife paired with a full belly lulls me into relaxation. Holding Leni's hand, I rest my head against hers.

"I never thought I'd be here," Leni states quietly.

"What do you mean?" I question with a smile.

"Living here, being with you, working on the ranch, swinging on a porch swing—all of it. You know?"

"Is 'all of it' a good thing?"

"Yeah, it is. It's just different."

"Do you miss New York?"

"You know, I thought I would miss it more." She chuckles. "Leaving was my dream for as long as I can remember, but the reality of it wasn't what I'd thought it would be. I'm happier now than I ever was in New York. Isn't that weird?"

"Not really," I scoff.

"I just wish I didn't have a slow learning curve," she states, absentmindedly tracing circles against my thigh.

"How's that?"

"It's taken me such a long time to find myself. It's like New York was a waste. I distanced myself from Texas to find happiness, but I didn't. I found massive student loan debt, shallow friendships, and no real growth. I mean, I returned every bit as broken as I was when I'd left."

"Yeah, but maybe you needed to experience a life away so that, when you returned, you could be open for growth and not always wondering about the what-ifs because you already know. You did everything you'd set out to do, and through those experiences, you realized that it wasn't what you needed. Plus, an education is never a waste. You're an amazing artist, Len, and a lot of your talent was learned in the city."

"I suppose you're right."

"I know I'm right. New York was part of your journey, and it led you back here."

"True."

I thread my fingers through Leni's and hold her hand as we rock.

My body tingles, and my desire pulsates through my veins as Leni's lips move against mine. I could make a career of this, spending the rest of my days lost in her lips, and I'd be completely happy. I muster all my willpower, and I pull away.

My eyes remain closed for a moment after the kiss has stopped, and I get my bearings. When I open them, I see her—my Leni girl. Her hooded eyes and lust-filled expression tell me that our kisses affect her in the same way they do me.

I clear my throat. "I have to get back to work," I say with little motivation behind my words.

"No. Stay here and kiss me."

She splays her hands across my chest, and I groan because my need for her has reached the point of uncomfortable.

"I can't, Len," I say, readjusting my jeans. I nod toward the window and the ranch beyond. "I have … stuff … to do." My hormone-muddled brain is barely able to make much sense of anything right now.

"Stuff?" she questions, raising an eyebrow. "Stuff doesn't sound too important. Stay with me. I need you," she pleads.

Hearing her say those last three words almost makes me comply. Yet I can't. We're not teenagers anymore, and mortgages aren't paid with kisses.

I shake my head. "You have work, and so do I." I motion to the pile of paperwork on the desk of my office.

I'm not sure exactly what it is, but Leni was intently going through it when I stopped by to see her a few minutes ago.

"My work can wait." She shrugs with a cheesy grin.

"Well, mine can't." I chuckle and lightly kiss her on the forehead before stepping back. "I'll see you in a little bit."

"Okay." She nods. "My lips will miss yours while you're gone."

"All of me will miss all of you."

I leave my office and walk out to my truck with a huge grin on my face.

The past few weeks with Leni have been nothing short of awesome. We've fallen into a comfortable routine. She works on ranch stuff for about half of the day and paints in her studio the other half. I visit her at both places when I can, and our lips get lost in one another. In fact, a lot of our time together is spent kissing. I just can't get enough of her.

The two of us always eat dinner with Mimi, and a few times a week, my parents join us. I think Mrs. Turner loves having the extra people around to feed. My parents love the time to see me. With ranch commitments and Leni, I haven't seen them as much lately.

Our evenings are spent walking around the open land, hand in hand, or tucked away in my makeshift bedroom in the barn, making out like crazed teenagers. If there were an Olympic medal for restraint, I would win gold, hands down.

I want Leni more than I want my next breath, but I haven't let it go all the way—yet. For some reason, I can't. I suppose, given our history, I'm just waiting for the ball to drop. I know I shouldn't be, but this girl has broken my heart several times before, and that isn't something I can forget. If I had Leni in every way possible, if I felt what it was like to be inside her, and then she ran, I don't know how I'd recover from that.

I know I'm being an idiot. The girl of my dreams, the one I've loved since I was young, is begging me to have sex with her on a daily basis, and I refuse. I'm not a prude when it comes to sex either. I barely knew the names of some of the girls I was with in college, yet that didn't stop me from screwing them. But Leni isn't just some girl; she's *the* girl. For me, she always has been, and the instant her beautiful greens, wide and surprised, greeted me in front of my truck a few months back, I knew she'd be mine. I just need her to *know* it, too.

She's still whispering dreams of leaving and making it out in the world. I want her to realize that she's my world, and it's crucial that I'm hers as well. I can't leave the ranch. This is what I'm meant to do with my life. Leni is meant to be an artist, no doubt. But she can be one here. She can have a beautiful life *here*. She needs to stop chasing happiness and just live in it.

"Oh my gosh!" Leni squeals, her eyes bright with excitement. "I haven't been here since ..." Her voice trails off as we both undoubtedly think of the last time Leni came to the river.

"Since you were thirteen," I answer for her, remembering everything about that day.

"Yeah." She nods. "Not a great memory, huh?"

"Don't sweat it. It was a long time ago. We're different people now. Plus, that wasn't the last time you stormed off on me. I kind of got used to it." I smile, nudging her in the side.

She turns to face me. "You kept coming back, every summer, multiple times. It was like you couldn't take a hint," she teases before her words ring more serious. "Why didn't you give up on me? I was so horrible to you."

"I could never give up on you. You were the answer to my dreams before I even knew to dream them. You were my favorite person in the world, and I just hoped that, if I tried hard enough, you'd come back to me."

"And I did," she says softly.

"Did you? Are you mine, Leni?" My voice lowers as I swipe a lock of her hair behind her ear and step in closer.

Her body leans in as her green eyes stare into mine. "I am."

My heart beats loudly at her words, and hope fills my chest. I want to believe her; I do. I wish I weren't waiting for something to go wrong, for the inevitable end ... but I am. Loving a girl like Leni over the years has given me some trust issues—at least, with her.

"I know we've only been dating for a few weeks, but I've known and loved you most of my life. I understand why I acted the way I did. I'm not the same person I was when I got here. I'm not the same girl I was in New York. I'm not the same girl I was when we were young. I'm not going to hurt you, Liam."

She wraps her arms around my neck, and we pull each other into an embrace.

I don't answer. Instead, I hold her against me. After a few beats, I step back and remove my shirt. I shake my head with a laugh when Leni ogles over my bare chest.

She quickly follows suit and removes her clothes until she's standing in her string bikini. Flashbacks to when I was fourteen enter my mind, except, this time, I don't have to hide the fact that her bikini-clad body turns me on.

"You are so gorgeous," I say before pressing my fingers against her waist and pulling her into a kiss. Reluctantly, I release her and reach down to the bag I brought, pulling out some sunscreen. "Would you like me to get your back?" I ask, holding up the bottle of SPF lotion.

"You even remembered sunscreen?" She shakes her head with a grin.

I shrug in acknowledgment. "I know that your shoulders burn easily."

Leni holds my stare with hers. She bites her lip and studies me, a thoughtful expression crossing her features. "You're too good, Liam."

She turns away from me and grabs her hair, pulling it to the side. After squirting some of the lotion in my hand, I rub it into her skin, my hands gliding over her back.

"Is 'too good' a compliment?" I drag my palms over her shoulders and down her arms.

She nods. "Absolutely."

"All right, then I'll take it." I pop the cap back onto the lotion and drop it into my bag.

We make our way to the old oak tree at the bank of the river. The rope that we used to swing from still hangs from a long branch.

"Are you sure this is safe?" Leni asks. "This rope has been here forever." She skeptically eyes it.

I give it a couple of hard tugs. "Completely safe. Want to wager a bet for old times' sake? See who can go further?" I ask, raising an eyebrow.

Leni's eyes light up, and she bites her lip with a nod of her head. "Hmm," she says, pressing her index finger against her lips. "I think we should. But what should it be?"

"Well, I think we've outgrown our wagers of the past." I chuckle, thinking back to some of the things we used to bet. I no longer have any interest in making Leni clean out a horse stall or have her give me the rest of her pack of gum.

"Definitely." She giggles before turning more serious. "But there is something I want that you aren't giving me."

Tingles run up my spine at the thought of being inside Leni. "You're going there?"

She nods. "Yep," she answers, making a popping sound at the end of the word.

"Okay, if I go further … you stay in Texas." I lay it all on the line.

"Liam," she sighs. The tone of her voice causes my hopes to plummet.

"Forget it." I wave my hand and smile. "Um … if I win, you buy me some gum—and not just any kind. Big League Chew."

"Oh my gosh! I haven't seen a pack of Big League Chew in years!" she exclaims. "I forgot all about our obsession with it. Do they still make it?"

I shrug. "Honestly, I'm not sure. But they have to, right?"

"I hope so. Though it's not going to matter since I'm going to beat you anyway." She shoots me a wink and reaches out her hand. "It's a deal then."

"It's a deal." I shake her hand.

I plant a quick kiss on her lips before jogging back a few feet and running toward the rope. I grab hold and swing in the air before releasing when the rope is at its highest point. When I surface from the water, I see Leni catch the rope. After ensuring that it stays still, she copies my previous movements and swings through the air with a shriek.

She rises from the water, a couple of feet in front of me. She's grinning wide as she swims a few strokes toward me and throws her arms around my neck. "So not fair," she protests.

"Oh, it's fair," I say as she circles her legs around my waist. "When we get back, you'd better start your search for my gum."

"You'll get your gum," she promises before her lips find mine.

We have just as much fun swimming in the river as we did when we were kids. Except, now, I can kiss her, and that makes it a hundred times better. And, if I ignore the nagging voice in my head, reminding me that she still wants to leave, I could say that I've never been happier.

Leni and I lie on our towels on the bank of the river, staring up through the leaves of a tree. The bright blue sky peeks through the swaying branches.

I sit up. "I have a surprise for you."

She crosses her legs and faces me. "What?" she asks eagerly.

"Well, I've been making some calls to a few friends from college. One of my friends knows the owner of an art gallery in downtown Austin."

Leni sits up straighter, her eyes going big. "Yeah?"

"So, I contacted the owner, Frank, and told him about your work. I sent him a few photos. He'd like to meet with you."

"You're lying! No way! What? When? Seriously?" she shrieks.

I throw my head back in laughter. "Seriously," I say through a grin. "I have his information back at the house. I'll give it to you when we go back. I'm not sure what will come of it, but it could be good, right?"

"Yes!" Pure joy radiates from Leni as tears roll down her cheeks. "It could be great!" She shakes her head. "I can't believe you did something like this for me. You're too good to me. This is so amazing. I just can't ..." She chokes on her words.

I lean in and swipe my thumb across her cheek. "I would do anything for you. I love you, Len."

"I love you, too," she says. "I don't deserve you, but I love you."

"You deserve everything. I'd give you the whole fucking world if I could," I tell her.

If only I could give her the world, then maybe she'd stay.

nineteen

Leni

I can barely breathe as I look around the beautifully lit space. This studio is simply gorgeous, and I'd be lying if I said that my framed pieces didn't make it even better.

Thanks to Liam's connection, I met with Frank a month ago with my portfolio in hand and my heart on my sleeve. I tried to play it cool, as if meeting with art gallery owners were a normal occurrence in my life. Thankfully, Frank made me feel so comfortable, and he truly loved my Texas-themed canvases, stating that he thought there was a huge market for them. I held in tears when he offered me my own show. Standing here now, with my work on the walls, I still can barely believe that it's real.

"I'm so proud of you, Leni girl," Mimi says beside me.

"Thank you for being here, Mimi."

"I wouldn't have missed it for the world, my girl. These are some of your best pieces to date, I do believe." Mimi nods her head in approval as she scans the room.

"I think so, too," I agree. "I guess Texas isn't all bad. Apparently, it makes for some great inspiration."

"Oh, my girl, you'll get there." She pats me on the back. "You'll get there."

I'm about to ask her about her meaning when Frank joins us.

"It's showtime," he tells me. "Are you ready?"

"Yes!" I've been waiting for this moment my entire life. *My own show!*

Frank heads to the front of the studio to open the doors. Liam appears and hands me a glass of wine.

"Thank you," I tell him as I take him in. I can't decide if he's more attractive in his Wranglers or the black suit he's wearing. "Gosh, you clean up nice. You are hot," I say before blushing when I realize that Mimi is still standing beside me.

"I'm going to walk around," Mimi says with a grin.

I can't help but laugh.

"And you look beautiful, as always." Liam softly kisses me. "I'm proud of you."

"Thank you," I tell him for probably the hundredth time.

"Knock 'em dead, baby." He squeezes my free hand before leaving my side.

I make my way toward the people now entering the studio.

I greet the guests as they come in. I thought I'd be more nervous than I am. Everyone is so nice and interested in hearing about my art, inspirations, and techniques. Turns out, it's really easy to talk about my own pieces. I know they're good, and I just feel proud.

"Oh, sugar, we need this one for the baby's room," a woman says in a thick Texan accent.

I walk over to her and her husband as they stand in front of the canvas that I named *Hope*.

"I love this one, too," I say to them.

It's one of the few non-landscape pieces that I have in the show. It's a close-up of the new calf's face with emphasis on her soft nose and deep brown eyes. Baby cows are one of the cutest animals in the world. It was fun to paint her.

"Oh, it's just darling. Are you the artist, dear?" the woman asks.

"I am."

"Such a fantastic job. Do you have any others of baby animals? A horse or a piglet?" she asks.

"My wife is obsessed with decorating the nursery with baby farm animals," the husband tells me with a chuckle, nodding toward her belly.

My eyes drop to the round belly that the woman has her hand on. "I don't, but I could paint some."

"Oh, I'd love that. We will definitely be getting this one, and I'd like to hire you to paint some more, if that's okay." She looks toward her husband. "Oh, sugar, I also want the one with the barn and the sunset over there. It will look great above our mantel. Go buy them before someone else does. Thank you, baby."

She takes my business card, and I take hers, promising to touch base this week about the other paintings she wants. The feeling is surreal. Someone is commissioning my work. It's unreal.

The night flies by in a blur. I talk so much that I feel like I'm about to lose my voice, and I've never felt happier. Frank is a true genius. He marketed the event so well, and traffic has been amazing the entire night.

"That, Leni, is what we call a success," he says with a grin after he closes the doors behind the last guests.

"Oh my gosh. It was, wasn't it?" I clap my hands together.

"We sold every piece." He smiles wide.

"No, we didn't." I cover my mouth.

He nods. "We did."

I start to jump up and down, and then I pull Mimi and Liam into a hug. The three of us hold on to each other for a few seconds. I'm so thankful that I got to share this moment, this life-changing day, with these two.

"I knew your work would go over well," Frank says. "You'd better get to painting. We need to set up another show."

"Okay, I can do that!"

I tell Frank how thankful I am for him several more times before Liam, Mimi, and I head out.

"Where should we go to celebrate?" Mimi asks.

"I know the perfect restaurant," Liam says.

I raise my hand in excitement. "My treat! This is, like, the first real money that I've made. I still can't believe it."

We hop in Liam's truck and drive a few minutes to the restaurant.

"Oh, valet parking. This place must be fancy," I say as Liam pulls up to the restaurant.

A nice gentleman holds his hand out for Mimi as she steps down from Liam's truck. He hands Liam a ticket as another valet drives up in a fancy sports car. I look at the shiny vehicle and can't help but think that my dad is probably driving a pretentious, midlife-crisis vehicle like that right now.

It's then that I hear it—his laugh. I'd know that deep chuckle anywhere. His laughter was a rarity when I was growing up, and the few times I heard it are ingrained in my brain. My eyes go wide when I see him. He's facing the outside of the restaurant, hunched over a woman. He has one arm around her waist and the other propped against the building.

My mouth drops open as I watch his lips work their way up her neck until they're engulfing her mouth in a kiss. He's always looked like one of those suckerfish on the side of an aquarium when he kissed my mom. I shudder at the thought.

There's just one big problem. This woman isn't my mother.

The two of them separate and turn toward the car loop where Mimi and I stand, motionless, staring in their direction.

My father startles when he sees us but regains his composure before his hooker friend even notices he lost it. He continues to hold her hand as he walks toward us. He pauses momentarily as he passes.

"Eleanora, Mother," he says with a curt nod before getting in his car and driving off.

I face Mimi, but no words come. She's just as speechless as I am, and her face looks so sad. I can understand why. I'd be devastated if that were my son. Then again, I'm equally as bummed that he's my father.

Liam asks if I'm okay.

"I ..." I try to answer him, but I don't know what to say. I reach for my purse and pull out my cell phone. I'm dialing my mom before I know it.

"Hello?" she answers.

"Where's Dad?" I blurt out.

"Eleanora?"

"Where's Dad?" I say again.

"He's out of town, on business. Why? Is something wrong?"

"Are you and Dad still together?"

"Eleanora, what's this about?" She sounds confused.

My voice shakes. "Are you and Dad still together?" I repeat.

"Of course we are. What's going on? Are you okay?"

I slowly shake my head even though she can't see me. Tears fall down my face. "You gave up everything for him, Mom, and he's evil. You put him first. You put a horrible person first. You lost me and everything else for a cheater."

I hang up before she can respond, but she doesn't call back, and I'm not surprised. Deep down, I know that he's probably never been faithful, and though I can't comprehend her reasons for loving him, I think she's always known.

I wrap my arms around Mimi, and she holds me as I cry. I don't know why I care about my parents. They've certainly never cared for me. Yet, somehow, this recent discovery makes everything worse, and my chest aches.

"I just want to go home, Liam. I'm sorry."

The drive back to Elkwood does nothing more than give my anger time to intensify. I'm twenty-three, and I still can't stop my parents and their horrible lives from affecting me. I can't fathom why I care. I'm living with my favorite person in the world and dating my other favorite person. I just had the best night of my career, and I can legitimately say that I'm happy. Then, I saw him, and it pulled me back into the darkness. And, now, to know that not only is he a horrible, judgmental, demanding, cold person ... but he's also unfaithful to a woman—albeit a weak one—who gave up everything for him, including me.

Regardless of how much I don't want to care about my parents, I still do. No matter how many times I tell myself that I don't need their approval, I still want it. And I hate that about myself the most.

twenty

Leni

"Fifty-three thousand five hundred twenty!" I shout my guess to the contestant on *The Price Is Right*. "Two hundred thousand? Are you stupid?" I yell at the man in the television who just gave his Showcase bid. "There's no way that could be two hundred thousand." I glare in disgust.

What a moron.

"Leni girl?" Mimi questions from a few feet away.

I mute the TV. "Yes?"

"Go outside."

Her command is said with a sweet tone because Mimi couldn't be anything but kind, but it still makes me do a double take.

"What?"

"Get off the couch, go outside, and get over it."

I squint toward her in question.

"I know you're in a funk, but, love, enough is enough. You've got to stop letting your parents affect you this way."

I sigh because I know she's right.

"Every day that you're given on this earth is a gift. You can't choose who your parents are or how they treat you. But you can choose how you're going to be in this life. You're an adult. Are you going to lie around on the sofa, feeling sorry for yourself, or are you going to go live?"

"Live." I let out a stubborn breath.

"You know I love you unconditionally, and I'm pretty sure that boy out there does, too. Yet everyone has a breaking point. Don't push him to his. He's not who you're mad at."

So, apparently, Mimi has noticed me avoiding Liam for the past few days. I don't even know why I've been avoiding him. It's true; I'm not mad at him. I'm just so used to shutting down when I feel this way.

God, I'm so tired of feeling this way.

"Okay, I'll go shower." I pass Mimi and squeeze her hand in thanks. "Love you."

"I love you, too."

My lips automatically turn up into a smile as I make my way out to the barn. I've missed Liam's kisses. I've missed Liam, period. I've only been in my self-induced pity party for a few days, but it's the longest I've gone without Liam's company for a couple of months now.

As soon as I enter the barn, I freeze. Liam's not alone. In fact, his arms are wrapped around a skinny little blonde's waist. She steps back from their embrace, and her perky little ponytail sways as she says something to make Liam laugh.

I can't even see her face, yet I know she's beautiful. My heart is pounding; the echoes ring so vibrantly in my ears that it's all I can hear. I can't make out Liam and the blonde's words, but I can see his face clearly, and it breaks me. He's happy. Whatever she's saying to him makes him happy. I see the adoration that he holds for her in his eyes, and that realization brings tears to mine.

Leave.

Turn around.

Go.

I can't make my legs move.

How could he do this to me?

He said he loved me, and I believed him. I'm such a fool, just like my mother.

Liam notices me, and panic immediately takes over his features. He's busted, and he knows it.

"Leni?" he says, concern lining his voice.

"I can't believe you," I say softly with a slow shake of my head.

I turn to leave.

"Leni, stop!" Liam yells.

My mind tells me to run, but my damn heart listens to him, and I stop. The sounds of Liam's footsteps against the ground get louder until he's right behind me. He takes my arm, and I turn to face him.

Liam lets out a sigh of relief. "Leni, you remember my cousin, Jenna, from California? You met her once or twice when we were young, I think."

My eyes dart to the confused blonde, who waves hesitantly in my direction. I haven't seen Jenna since I was eight or nine maybe, but I recognize her face. I wave back with a weak smile, too embarrassed to say anything.

Liam turns to Jenna. "Can you head home? I'll meet up with you in a bit."

Jenna walks out of the barn like a woman on a mission, and I don't blame her. I'd want to get away from me, too.

"I'm sorry," I say to Liam. "I just saw her, and I thought ..."

"I know what you thought." He sighs. "Listen, I can't do this." He starts to leave.

"Wait! What do you mean, you can't do this?" I stare at him and can't believe how much I love him and how beautiful he is to me. My entire body wants to run to him and kiss him until I'm dizzy, but I've gone and messed things up again.

"I need time to think, Leni." He sounds defeated.

"About us? Why?"

He lets out a dry chuckle. "Why? Because I don't know what to do anymore. I try so hard with you, Len. I love you. I'm patient, supportive. I do everything in my power to make you happy, and you are for a while, but something always happens to pull you from me."

He runs his hands through his hair in frustration. "It's like I'm living in a perpetual cycle of fear with you, always waiting for something to go wrong, for you to run. I love you too much to live every day, afraid of losing you." He looks toward the direction of his father's farm. "And Jenna? You thought I was cheating on you? I've been in love with you since we were teenagers, and you actually thought that I'd cheat on you? That I had it in me to do something like that? Sometimes, I feel like you don't see me at all."

"I said I was sorry," I plead.

"I'm not your father, Len. Not even close, yet I feel like you're constantly waiting for me to turn into him. I can't make you love me, and I can't make you stay. I'm not strong enough to love you, knowing that you'll leave."

"I love you. You know I do," I tell him.

"Not enough." He shakes his head. "You need to grow up some more, Leni. Your emotions are all over the place. Sometimes, you're this smart, driven artist, and the next minute, you act like an emotionally stunted teenager. I feel like I've been fighting with you to love me for half of my life. I can't do it anymore."

I see the conflict in his stare. He wants me right now, just as much as I want him ... yet he still turns to leave again.

"Wait!" Suddenly, everything is crystal clear, and maybe it's been for a while, but like Mimi always says, I just keep getting in my way. I can't be my own worst enemy anymore.

"Listen," I beg, "I know I'm difficult, Liam. I wish I weren't. God, I wish I were a normal chick with normal problems, but I'm not. Do you know why I pushed you away that summer at the river when I was thirteen? It's because, in that moment, I realized I loved you—and not just friend love. I knew that I was in love with you and always would be. I knew that I'd stay for you, and I couldn't."

I move my head from side to side. Liam's stance softens, and I continue, "You know about my childhood and my parents, but I don't think you understand how much it truly affected me. I saw my mother turn into this shell of a person, all because she loved my father. I felt suffocated my entire childhood, and I wanted to escape. I didn't want to let love ruin me, like it ruined her. I was afraid to lose myself. I was afraid to love you. I was terrified of becoming my mother. I'd rather live a life of loneliness than to ever know what it felt like to walk in her shoes. That was my biggest fear. And I realize that all love isn't like that, and I had a shitty example of what love means. But it's what I knew. So, I pushed you away to save myself."

I take a step toward Liam, and he follows suit until we're standing right across from each other.

I hold his hands in mine. "I had this ill-conceived notion that I had to do certain things in life to find happiness. And I *needed* to be happy, Liam. More than anything. Yet, no matter how much I searched for joy or did things I thought would lead me there, it never came. I did everything in my power to leave Texas, and I still ended up back here anyway. I've been trying to be happy my entire life. Yet I've finally realized that everything I need has been here all along. The truth is that my heart has always been here, on this farm. It's always belonged to you."

Liam bends and presses his forehead against mine as I continue, "Liam, I loved you before I knew what love was. I loved you then, and I love you now. There is no one on this earth who could ever love me the way you do, and the way you love me is perfect. I'm done with pushing you away. I'm done with running. I'll never find what I'm looking for anywhere else. I'm destined to live my life in Elkwood, with you, and I'm done with pretending that I'm not." I cradle his face in my hands.

He studies me with longing in his eyes.

"I know I'm hard to love. I know I'm immature and idiotic at times. I get it. I can't lose you though, Liam. Just give me time to figure out this new normal. I don't want to be the Leni of my past. I want to be the Leni who is secure and happy and doesn't let the ghosts of her youth dictate her future. I want to be the Leni who shows you every day just how much I love you. Please believe me."

His hands grasp at my waist. "I do, Len."

"Okay." My voice cracks. I pull in a few calming breaths. "So, you don't need to think?"

He chuckles softly. "I don't need to think. I've known for a long time that I'd never love another the way I love you. You've been my everything, all I've ever needed. I simply needed you to feel it, too."

"I'm sorry it took me so long."

"You were worth the wait, Leni."

Liam holds me against him, and I snuggle my face against his chest. I can't help but think about all the time I wasted, running, searching for something I already had. In that way, I am a fool. I can't change the past, but I'll never make the same mistakes again. I truly know this now.

twenty-one

Liam

I feel the tension leave Leni's body as I hold her. The walls that she put up are gone. She's finally mine.

Damn, that feels good.

I always hoped she'd come around, and despite everything, I believed that she would. Admitting to a life without her was too painful. So, I held on to hope.

She tilts her head back, and her bright green eyes capture mine, a content smile resting on her lips. She's so incredibly beautiful, and I know that I'm going to be staring at this gorgeous face for the rest of my life.

I softly kiss her, slowly moving my lips against hers. Feeling her, tasting her, loving her—it's all I've ever wanted. She threads her fingers through my hair, and a shiver runs through me. I deepen the kiss, wanting more, needing everything.

Without removing my lips from hers, I walk us back toward the bedroom I had built and shut the wooden door behind us. It's not much, but it's clean, private, and here. And I can't wait another minute to be with Leni.

Once inside the bedroom, our kisses become frantic. We make quick work of removing our clothes. My hands roam her body as hers return the favor. She feels incredible. Her skin is smooth, and her body is perfect. She slides her palms across my shoulders, down my chest, and over my abs, searing me with her touch. She moans, and I sigh, our bodies quivering.

Her hands explore below my waist and grab ahold of me just as my fingers find her warmth.

"Oh, fuck," I groan.

"Oh my God," Leni cries as we continue to pleasure one another.

I'm cognizant of nothing, yet I feel everything. The pleasure extends through every nerve cell, and every inch of my body vibrates with sensation.

This is unlike anything I've ever experienced, and I never want it to end. My mouth pays homage to Leni's breasts, my tongue enjoying each of her nipples, as my fingers work below. She starts to shake and rock against my hand. Throwing her head back, she moans into the hormone-induced space. She tightens around my fingers, and I watch as she falls apart. Her head falls back, and she cries out as her body quivers.

It's the single sexiest thing I've ever seen in my life.

I lay her down on the bed as she comes down from the high. I reach for a condom from the bedside table and put it on. Lying atop her, I take both of her hands in mine and thread our fingers together. Our joined hands rest on either side of Leni's head on the pillow. I lightly kiss her lips and pull my face away from hers just slightly. Our gazes lock, and I watch her face as I enter her.

I want to remember this moment and everything about it forever. I've dreamed of being with Leni since I was probably too young to be thinking such thoughts to begin with.

Our eyes remain locked as I pick up the pace. As she bites her lip, Leni's eyes are hooded, but she doesn't close them.

I want to kiss her, but I want to watch her more. Seeing her body's reaction to our connection is as good as being inside her. Almost.

Damn, she's everything.

We make love. It's soft and hard. Frenzied and slow. There are moments of unabashed sounds coming from our lips and then seconds where the only noise is our skin hitting against one another. It's all I've ever wanted and so much more than my best dreams.

It's with Leni, and I don't ever want to be with another woman in this lifetime. Now that I've had her, there's no going back.

Leni's eyes roll back, and her whimpers grow more intense. I chase my release as she finds hers. And then there's only pleasure.

I lie beside Leni on the bed. We're breathing heavily as we stare at the barn ceiling.

"Oh my God," Leni says, breathless.

"Agreed." I squeeze her hand in mine.

She props herself up on her elbow and looks at me. "You were so worth the wait."

I chuckle. "Good. But there's no more holding out anymore. We're going to be doing that a lot more often."

"Uh, yeah … like, every day," she agrees.

"And twice on Sundays."

She blows out a puff of air. "Or more."

I lift my hand to her cheek. "So, you're really mine?"

"I'm completely yours, Liam," she says with sincerity.

"No more running."

"I'm never leaving you again. I promise."

"I love you, Len."

"I love you, Liam."

She lowers her head, and her lips find mine once more.

twenty-two

Liam

*L*eni sits on the floor of her studio, her legs out to her side. She's wearing a flowy sundress, a pale yellow, like the first rays of sunshine that warm the earth each morning. Her locks, the color of sweet cinnamon, are curled, cascading over her shoulders in waves. The bright sun streams in through the windows, seemingly pointed directly on her, showcasing her in light. In profile, she looks like a Grecian goddess.

My goddess.

She hasn't noticed me yet, and I'm glad. I welcome the stolen moment, appreciating all that she is—all that's now mine. I love watching her in her element. There's a certain quality a person who is truly happy radiates, and I think that Leni is filled with joy, maybe for the first time in her life. The best part is that she finally realizes it. She no longer thinks this is simply a pit stop on her journey. In the whole scheme of things, it hasn't been that long since Leni came back into my life, and yet the change in her is obvious, so palpable that I can feel the happiness in this space on my skin like a soft blanket, comforting and safe. It wasn't that long ago that walking into a room with Leni felt like entering an ice box, the air frigid enough to steal one's breath.

The long brush in her hand flicks lightly against the canvas before her, a soft jade accenting the leaves of a tall oak. She tilts her head to the side to study her work, seeing details that only she as the artist is privy to.

Sometimes, I still can't believe that she's mine, and we're happy.

I'm not sure why, but deep down, I always believed we'd end up together. Despite every horrible thing we've been through, I could never love someone else the way in which I love her. From the first moment I met her, a young girl with a fiery spirit, she became my other half, someone I cherished, valued, needed in my life. At an age where I'd recently learned how to write my last name by myself or tie my shoes without making the laces into bunny ears first, I still realized that Eleanora Turner was something special, someone that I wanted in my life in more ways than I could fully grasp at the time.

As I watch her now, nostalgia pulls me in. Memories of everything we were, went through, and lost to end up here play across my heart, and I feel so lucky to have made it to this point. All the stages of my life have been shaped and molded into our current reality because her existence was so deeply embedded in who I was, who I am.

My thoughts drift to an important milestone, though it's one I don't enjoy dwelling on—the day I grew up, largely because of Leni, on my seventeenth birthday, one of the worst days of my life. Yet that day forced me to stand tall and keep going, even when I wanted to crumble. The thing is that life isn't always wonderful, but one's got to suck it up and move on. The world isn't going to stop because I'm hurting.

And it didn't stop. Leni broke my heart, more than she ever had, and I had to take a deep breath and go help my dad on the ranch with the realization that I might never see Leni again. I didn't have a choice, and that feeling of uncertainty is humbling and scary as hell. But, every day since, I've gotten up each morning and put one foot in front of the other regardless of whether I wanted to or not.

Leni's moment happened much later, perhaps because of the environment in which she had been raised, her stubbornness, or a combination of the two. I don't think she truly grew up until recently, and it wasn't all at once. I think there've been many pivotal moments over the past year that Leni needed in order to turn into the person she was destined to be, starting with losing everything and having to leave New York and finally culminating in the barn when she realized that she might actually lose me.

Every day isn't perfect. By nature, we'll always be imperfect, as all people are, but it's as close as it can be. Additionally, for the first time in my life, I'm not waiting for the ball to drop. I'm not afraid of something happening that will cause her to leave. I know she's mine, and I know she always will be.

Leni looks up from her painting, noticing me in the doorway. "Oh, hey. Are we ready to go?"

"Yep." I nod and push off of the doorframe. "Mimi just finished packaging up the food." I eye the canvas in front of her. "I thought that one was finished?"

Leni stands and peers down at the picture of a beautiful Texas landscape. "I thought so, too, but it needed a little more dimension on the leaves of the tree." She drops her paintbrush into the cup of liquid by the easel. "But it's good now."

She grins and closes the gap between us. When she reaches me, she drapes her arms around my neck, and her full lips press against mine. Her tongue licks at my lips, searching for entry, and I willingly comply. I take the kiss deeper, exploring all the ways in which our tongues can move together. I could kiss Leni all day.

A quiet sigh escapes her lips when I finally pull away.

"Do we have to go?" she protests.

"Yes." I let out a chuckle.

"Fine, but we shall resume this later." She smacks my ass before leading the way downstairs.

I grab the dishes from Mimi, and the three of us hop into my truck.

A short drive later, we're in town at Emily and Westley's house.

"Where would you like the food Mrs. Turner made?" I ask Westley as we enter the foyer.

"On the table is fine. Thanks," he tells me before extending a hug to Mimi and thanking her for the dishes.

I steal a glance at Leni as she smiles at her grandmother, so much pride radiating from her.

Mrs. Turner is known as one of the best cooks in our small town, and she never passes up an opportunity to share her talent with others. You sneeze too loud, and you're bound to receive a casserole from her. Food is definitely her love language, and she hands it out like candy. She has a lot of love to give. Leni is really Mrs. Turner's only real family left besides Leni's parents, though no one counts them. Yet she's one of the most cherished members of our community. Family isn't just those you're related to by blood; it's the people one surrounds themselves with, the ones they love.

As I place the ceramic dishes on the table, I hear the high shrills of adoration coming from the living room. It's the call of women and babies.

Stepping into the living room, I see Leni with a bundle in a pink crocheted blanket cradled in her arms. She's gazing down toward the soft pile with utter amazement in her eyes. I step closer, so I'm able to see the tiny human who's garnering all the affection. She's adorable, as most babies are. Though, to me, the most beautiful creature in this space is Leni. She's mesmerizing, and seeing her like this—happy, carefree, and content— makes her more gorgeous than ever.

God, I love her.

"Do you want to see her?" Leni motions toward the infant.

"She's precious." I nod.

"Isn't she?" she says before directing her words toward Emily, who is resting, looking a little tired, in the recliner. "She's just incredible, Em. Beyond perfect."

"She is," Emily agrees. "Though she'd be a tad more perfect if she slept for more than forty-five minutes at a time." She chuckles softly.

"What's her name again?" I ask.

"Sadie Mae," Westley states from beside me.

I chat with Westley as Mimi and Leni continue to gush over Sadie, taking turns in holding the baby.

"We'd better get going," Mimi states. "I know you two must be exhausted. We don't want to overstay our welcome. We just wanted to bring you some food and meet the little angel."

"Thank you, Mrs. Turner. So much," Emily says while pulling Mimi into a hug and kissing her cheek.

On our way out, we run into Pete and Melody heading toward the house. Melody holds a bouquet of flowers in her hands, and Pete holds their baby boy.

"Fancy seeing you here." Melody chuckles. "How's little Sadie?"

"Amazing," Leni answers. "Though Emily looks tired."

Melody shakes her head. "Oh, don't I know that feeling?" She shoots a faux glare toward her little one in her husband's arms. "They're lucky they're so cute. Well, we won't stay long. Just wanted to give our congratulations."

As Leni helps Mimi into the truck, I pull Pete aside. "Hey, man. Can you give me a call sometime this week? I'm ready to move forward with the house."

"Nice. Absolutely." He grins knowingly. "It will be great. Talk to you soon."

Leni lies atop me, my arms circled around her middle. Her head rests against my chest as we use a pile of straw as a bed. Leni traces lazy circles across the skin of my arm. The scent of the fresh straw beneath us and Leni's fruity body wash creates a heady sensation of happiness and lust within me. I love these moments of quiet. There are no words, just the feeling of Leni in my arms paired with the sounds of the ranch—my utopia.

I know I should break the spell and go do some work, but I can't make myself move from this spot. Seeing Leni hold that baby this morning was one of the biggest turn-ons. I can't wait to make a baby with her. All in good time. I realize I should probably propose and marry her first though. It's conflicting—wanting to enjoy every second and take it slow and wanting to start forever right now. I'm confident that everything I've ever wanted with Leni is possible, so I know there's no need to rush through it. I can't lie and say that thinking of her taking my name—Leni Moore—doesn't make me want to marry her today.

"What are you thinking about?" Leni asks on cue.

"Marrying you."

"Oh, yeah?" I can hear the smile in her voice.

"Oh, yeah." My voice is low, gravelly, and full of need.

I brush her hair off of her shoulder and kiss her neck, biting gently. Leni sighs, leaning deeper back into me.

"I love you, Leni Turner," I whisper between kisses.

"I love you," she says on an exhale.

I slide my hands down her side, the thin fabric of her sundress the only barrier between my palms and her soft skin. Grabbing the material, I pull, wadding it up in my hands until I've dragged it up to her chest. My hands glide across the taut skin of her abdomen and then down, dipping a finger between the band of her panties. She pulls in a deep breath.

I allow my finger to linger, lightly tracing back and forth where the elastic meets her skin. She grinds back into me, her ass pressing against my hard length beneath my jeans. I move my hands up until I reach her bra. With one movement, I snap it up, exposing her perfect breasts. I groan and grind into her from behind as my teeth tug on her ear.

She whimpers as my hands cup her breasts before I work her nipples between my fingers. Her head presses firmly into my collarbone as she moves against me. Each brush of her backside against my jeans sends a thrilling need up my spine.

Leaving her breasts, I trail my hands down her stomach, wanting to brand her with my touch, making her mine forever. Reaching her legs, I push her knees out to the side, so she's wide open, and this time, when my hand reaches beneath her panties, it keeps going until my fingers are in her warmth.

She's so wet and ready. Her breaths are frantic and needy as she moans out my name.

"Liam," she groans into the air as my fingers work inside her.

"Yes, baby?" I whisper into her ear.

"Liam," she says on a sigh that almost sounds pained.

I know what she wants, and I want to give it to her. I pull my fingers out of her, pulling her wetness up to the spot where she needs me most. I quickly rub against her bundle of nerves while my mouth kisses her exposed neck, and my pelvis grinds into her, desperate for relief.

"Liam," she cries as my fingers work faster.

I use my free hand to tug on her nipple while my fingers below rub firmly. Leni lifts her pelvis, pressing herself harder into my hand, desperate for release. Her legs start to shake, and her body follows. Every inch of her quivers as she cries out my name, a guttural sound that makes me want to explode.

As soon as Leni's body stops quivering, she stands and steps out of her soaked panties. I unzip my pants and pull them down, so I'm ready. Leni straddles me and slides down on my hard shaft. Closing my eyes, I lean my head back into the straw on a heated sigh. She always feels so amazing, so perfect, and so mine. I grab her hips and guide her, and she bounces up and down on me.

I'll never get enough of her for as long as I live.

I'll always want more.

More Leni.

More sex.

More everything.

Leni presses her forehead against mine. Our collected breaths are loud, our sweaty bodies coming together again and again and again. She rides me fast and hard, chasing pleasure.

We reach our destinations together. Just as she starts to shake, I come hard. I capture my name from her lips as she screams.

Still connected to me, she falls onto me, and I wrap her in my arms. Our hearts pound beneath our chests. I kiss the top of her head and pull the hair off of her slick cheek.

The itchy straw sticking to my damp thighs so annoyingly reminds me that we desperately need to shower. But I can't bring myself to release my grasp on Leni just yet.

Twenty-three

Leni

"Admit it," I say with a grin under the spray of the shower. "You installed this room and bathroom, so you could shower after getting laid. Didn't you?" The warm water hits my face, and I wipe it from my eyes, not wanting to miss a second of the view.

I find everything about Liam attractive, but there's something about him all wet and slippery that's simply candy for my eyes. He's the most beautiful man I've ever seen, inside and out.

Liam's lips turn up into a smile, his fingers rubbing shampoo into his hair. "No. I told you why. It was just easier because I'm always here. You're the first girl to shower in my barn, Len."

I pucker my lips, quirking up an eyebrow. "Really? You promise?"

"I promise."

"So, you've never fucked another girl in this barn?"

His lips turn up with a sexy grin. "Just you," he says as he takes his soapy hands and quickly pulls down on my nipples before releasing them.

Startled, I yelp in surprise.

"And you'll be the only girl I'll ever make love to here or anywhere else," he promises me.

"You're such a romantic," I tease, running my hands up his chest.

I love the feel of his firm muscles underneath my touch. Liam is all muscle, and it's the muscle that one gets from hard work. He doesn't spend hours lifting at the gym, and yet his defined chest would rival anyone who does. His physique is a result of his passion for what he does, working fiercely to be the best in his field. He's determined and strong.

I work my hands from his chest to his abdomen before he grabs my wrist.

"I wouldn't go any further if I were you," he warns.

"Or what?"

"Or we won't be leaving this shower anytime soon."

I twist my wrist from his grasp and move my hand further down. I wrap my fingers around his shaft, which is hard and ready for me. "Then, I guess we won't be leaving this shower anytime soon."

I can't wipe the obnoxious grin from my face as I throw a clean T-shirt over my head. I was finally able to break free from my fascination with Liam for long enough to come inside for some clean clothes. I wonder how it looks to Mimi that I return from the barn every day freshly showered, only to go upstairs and change into some new clothes. Surely, she realizes what's going on, but she thankfully never says anything. As passionate as Mimi is about life and loving everyone who's in hers, I'm sure she was the same with my pops, not that I want to think about it in detail. There are some things in life that I just don't want to imagine. I bet I'm very similar to Mimi when she was my age. I had to inherit some of my spirit from her. Goodness knows I didn't get it from my mother.

Though, seriously, Liam and I can't help it. I'm officially obsessed with him. It's nearly impossible for me to keep my hands off him, especially when he's working, sweating, and doing manly things. He's hot—and not like how a lot of guys are attractive. He's the most gorgeous guy I've ever seen, and even from age thirteen, I knew I wouldn't be able to resist him. Thankfully, I don't have to anymore.

Mimi's landline rings downstairs, causing me to smile as I think about how much I've changed these past months. I love it here now in the world of landlines, three-channel TV, homemade bread, and barn sex. It's so vastly different from my life in New York, the life I thought I needed to be happy. I was so lost most of my life. I've truly just found myself and experienced what it means to be happy.

"Leni girl," Mimi calls from downstairs, and a shiver runs down my spine at the sound of her voice.

I finish zipping up my shorts and open my bedroom door.

I hurry down the stairs where Mimi is waiting. "Yeah?" I ask.

"Um, well … that was your mother on the phone. Your father had a heart attack."

Mimi's words resonate in my mind, but I have a hard time registering their meaning.

A heart attack?

The words clash with everything my father is. Though he's evil and hardheaded, he's strong. I can't imagine anything bringing him down, least of all his own body.

"He's in the hospital. Your mom thinks he'll recover, but we should go visit him." Mimi's voice is void of emotion, which is unsettling to me. She must still be internalizing the news she just received.

"Yeah, okay," I agree.

I call Liam to let him know what happened and that Mimi and I are making a trip to Dallas to see my Dad. Thirty minutes later, Mimi and I have an overnight bag packed and are on the way to the hospital.

It's challenging, trying to decipher my feelings. I know I should be sad and upset for my dad, but then there's that part of me that hates him, and though I would never wish ill on him, it's hard to find it in me to care either. The quietest part holds out hope that this is what we need to heal. Perhaps this will be an eye-opener for both of my parents—forcing them to see that life is short and recognize the value of having a relationship with their only daughter.

Will he apologize to me? Make amends? I'm not positive I even want that. There's so much hurt and anger when it comes to my parents. I know I'd find it hard to move past it all.

But they're my parents.

As much as I want to hold on to my rage forever, I want to be loved more.

Mimi and I walk hand in hand through the hallways of the hospital. The lights are bright, and everything smells of cleaner and sickness. It's nauseating. I'd rather be anywhere but here. I wish my father were at home, healthy as a horse and being his usual asshole self. One, because, despite everything he put me through, I don't want him to hurt. I would never wish pain on my mom or dad. And two—and honestly the main reason—is because I don't want to see him. I'm utterly terrified to be in his presence.

My mom greets us outside of his hospital room. She's well put together, even at a time like this. Her white linen pantsuit is wrinkle-free and tailored to perfectly hug every curve of her body. She has her hair tied up in a flawless French twist. She's wearing pearl stud earrings. Her makeup is immaculate—enough to highlight her natural beauty, but not too much as to draw attention away from Father in his time of need. I know all too well that, regardless of whether my father is at the hospital or healthy as a horse, back home in his office, it's always *his* time of need. This is my father's world, and we're all just living in it. My mom plays the role of the beautiful and obedient wife to the letter.

However, I can see details that no one else would pick up on. The area under her eyes is a shade darker than the rest of her skin, indicating the bags of worry that her foundation has covered up, almost seamlessly. The bobby pins in her hair are noticeable, off color from the ones she normally wears. In a haste to leave the house, she probably forgot to pack her own and had to resort to buying these off-brand ones at the drugstore down the street. The smile she wears is tight, as fake as the one she always wears, but her bottom lip quivers as she holds in tears.

Yeah, to the average person, my mom would appear to be the picture of perfection, but I know that, inside, she's falling apart. Her entire world is lying in a hospital bed, and she's barely holding it together. There's a piece of me that feels sorry for her. Despite her lack of love for me, she has love in spades for my father. I can only imagine how much I'd be hurting if something happened to Mimi or Liam. I'd be drowning in pain, and I suppose that's how my mother is feeling now.

She gives us the update on his condition, her voice as strong and chipper as it is when she introduces a charity that they're supporting at one of their benefits.

Ever the perfect wife.

According to my mother, he was in his study earlier today on the phone with another politician and just fell to his knees. She says she knew something was wrong when she heard his yelling stop from the kitchen. It's pretty telling that the thing that cued my mom into the fact that something was wrong was my father's lack of yelling at the person on the other line.

She tells us that the doctor thinks he'll be fine, and with some diet and medication changes, he should be back to himself in no time.

Well, that's a bummer.

My heart starts to beat rapidly, and I cling to Mimi's hand as we enter the room. I'm startled when I see him. The man lying on the bed is just a shell of my father. He looks pale and has more wrinkles than I've ever seen. His mouth droops down into a frown as he sleeps. It's unsettling, seeing this weak man before me and realizing that he's the one I've been running from all this time. Lying in front of me, he doesn't seem that terrifying.

He opens his eyes, and his beady pupils focus in on me as I stand next to his bed.

"Hi, Dad," I say quietly.

He blinks once. Twice. Then, he looks to my mom, and even in his weakened state, there's a demand there.

"Oh, right," my mom says softly and brings a cup of water toward his face, bending the straw to his lips. "Here you are, sweetie."

After he takes a drink, he flicks his hand, dismissing my mom.

He clears his throat. "Eleanora." My name sounds gruff, coming from his lips, and just like that, this weak man is once again my father, intimidating and cold.

"How are you feeling?" I ask him.

He doesn't answer my question. Instead, his gaze darts between Mimi and me. "I saw you in Austin."

"Yeah, I had an art show there. We were heading to dinner to celebrate." I turn to Mimi, and she nods approvingly.

"Art?" he questions.

"Yes, I finished my degree in art up in New York. That's what I do now." I force a smile, willing him to just accept me.

He shakes his head so subtly that it's barely noticeable, but I see it just the same.

"Pathetic," he whispers.

I squeeze Mimi's hand, the lump in my throat making it hard for me to breathe. My heart beats rapidly in my chest, and my eyes well with unshed tears. Everything about this, except for the fact that my father is in a hospital bed, takes me back to what I felt every single day, living with him as a child. With one word, he's crushed me—again. I was stupid to hope that him almost dying would change anything. He's too stubborn and set in his ways to change. He'll go to his grave, hating me and everything I stand for. I was naive to think otherwise.

"She's quite talented, Henry. She has a real gift, if you'd take the time to see it," Mimi says, her voice calm but strong.

In this moment, I love Mimi even more. She's always stood up for me, in ways that even my own mother never has.

"I suppose she's living with you?" he asks with a roll of his eyes.

Mimi smiles. "Yes, she is. It's wonderful to have her back."

He glares at Mimi before directing his vacant eyes to me, holding me in his stare. "You failed. Just like I knew you would. Now, you have to live with your grandma." He closes his eyes before saying, "Always an embarrassment."

I don't have time to register a response or reaction before Mimi stands tall beside me, addressing my father in a way that says she isn't remotely intimidated by him, "The only embarrassment is you, Henry. I'm glad your father isn't here to see the man you've turned out to be. It would break his heart." She shakes her head, and fury lines her voice. "You don't know Leni. You've never cared enough to know her. If you had, you'd realize that she's amazing. I feel sorry for you. You have an incredible daughter, and you'll never know her. It's such a shame. Pitiful," she says the last word with such disdain. "I love you, Henry. I want you to find happiness. We're only given one life, and it kills me that you're choosing to spend yours like this. But I can't stand around and let you crush this girl's spirit for one more second. Good-bye."

Mimi releases a long breath. "Come on, my girl. Let's go home," she says to me, her words soft and loving.

Being in a room with my parents for the first time in years, it hits me that I will never be in a room with the two of them again, and I know it.

This is it.

I reassuringly squeeze Mimi's hand before letting it go, Mimi's love giving me more strength than I've ever felt.

I turn to face my mom, addressing her first, "You know he's cheating on you, right? We saw him with a woman in Austin, but you probably already knew that, didn't you?"

My mom's eyes go wide.

"He's probably always cheated on you, hasn't he?"

She doesn't answer, but the fraction of a second that her armor fails and she lowers her gaze, I know it to be true. She's always known about his infidelities.

"He cheats on you, treats you like his servant, and has stopped you from having a life of your own. He forced you to give up your dreams for him, and you did it, no questions asked." My voice shakes with sadness. "That's not love, Mom. That's ownership. He doesn't love you. He's never loved anyone but himself.

"But I loved you, and I desperately wanted you to love me back. I needed my mom to love me." A tear falls down my cheek. "You chose him. Every single time."

I look between my parents. My dad glares at me with hatred, and my mom peers at me through shame-filled eyes.

"The two of you almost ruined me. Almost." I shake my head. "But you didn't."

Tears fall fast down my cheeks now, but they aren't ones of sadness or despair; they're tears of gratitude.

Because they didn't; they didn't break me.

"You didn't break me. You made me stronger. And Mimi loves me." I turn my focus to my grandma, who's silently crying beside me, her lips quivering in a grin. "And Liam loves me, and finally, I've learned to love myself. I'm happier than the two of you will ever be. So, you know what?" I pin each of them with a stare.

I gaze into my mother's eyes. "I forgive you. I forgive you for not loving me or yourself enough. I hope that, someday, you can find the courage to do just that."

I shift my attention to my dad, who continues to scowl in his hospital bed. "I forgive you, Dad. I forgive you for hurting me, for hating me, and everything in between. I'll never forget what you've done, but your wrongs no longer hold a place in my heart. Your heart possesses enough hate for the both of us, and clearly, it's destroying you. Good-bye."

The last sentiment is directed at them both, and I know that this is my final good-bye to these two. They won't change, and I won't let their poison affect me anymore. I no longer claim them as family of mine.

"Let's go home, Mimi." I wrap my arm around her waist, and the two of us walk out of that room without a backward glance.

The second we step outside, the air feels lighter, and I can take in a full breath again. I will never again be in a space so suffocating, and my chest fills with joy.

The fact of the matter is that my parents are awful. They always have been. I have no idea how someone as good and pure as Mimi had a son like my father. Some people are just born evil. It's not her fault. I know the way she loves, and I know she loved him the way a mother should love her child. He was just destined to be no good.

When I told my parents that I forgave them, I meant it. I do. I forgive every wrong they've ever done against me. The thing about forgiveness is, it's a gift to yourself. My forgiveness won't change their lives. They'll continue to be miserable all the rest of their days. But it will be life-changing for me. They hurt me for a long time. Why would I let the memories of that pain continue to hurt me forever? I'm letting it go. I'm stopping the cycle of pain. I'll never forget what they've done. But their wrongs have no place in my heart. I need all the space I have for love because I have a lot of it to give.

twenty-four

Leni

The paper feels so fragile between my fingers, and I'm terrified to move in fear of ripping it. Yet it's real—my first check for a commissioned piece of artwork. It's surreal. I can hardly believe it, yet I hold the proof in my grasp. Someone paid me to paint a piece for them.

A woman who purchased one of my Texas landscape paintings at my show in Austin wants me to create a similar piece, though on a much larger scale, for the sizable lobby of her law firm. It will be the biggest piece I've ever painted, and this check is the most I've ever received for my work.

"Everything okay?" Liam's voice is etched with concern.

I pull my stare from the check to meet his gaze. "Yes, more than okay." I give him a reassuring smile. "I'm in awe really. I've dreamed of this moment my whole life—

having someone who wants me to create art for them. I just want to remember what it feels like."

Liam crosses his arms and leans up against the frame of my bedroom door, a smile on his face. "You know this is just the first of many commissioned pieces. You'll have this again."

I shrug. "I really hope so. The show in Austin and now this—my dreams are coming true." I breathe in deep before adding, "Thanks to you."

I owe all of this to Liam. He's the one who bought me all of the supplies so that I could start painting again and put me in touch with Frank, which led to the show in Austin, which allowed this woman to see my paintings in the first place. The irony of it all isn't lost on me. I pushed Liam away for years, terrified that he'd kill my dreams. Yet, now, he's the reason they're coming true.

"This is all you. All of it. You've always been incredibly talented, and you're finally getting recognition for it. You deserve every bit of praise that comes your way."

I don't respond because, honestly, I feel like crying with gratitude, and I don't want to mess up my makeup.

"You look beautiful." Liam pushes off of the doorframe and closes the distance between us. His strong hands take hold of my waist before his lips find mine.

"You clean up nicely yourself," I tell him, my forehead pressed against his, breathing him in.

"Is Mimi ready?" he asks.

"She should be." I kiss him again before taking a step back. Grabbing my bracelet from the dresser, I lay it across my wrist. "Do you mind?" I ask Liam, nodding toward the small chain of silver resting on my skin.

He takes each end of the bracelet and clasps it for me.

"You think she suspects anything?" He lifts my hand toward his face, pressing his lips against the thin skin of my inner wrist, right above the silver clasp, before releasing my hand.

"Not a thing." I shake my head. "I did good. I didn't give anything away."

"Good."

I take one final peek in the mirror above my dresser and follow Liam down to the living room.

Mimi sits on the sofa, knitting a baby-blue blanket, no doubt for someone in town, who's expecting a little boy. "You ready for dinner, Mimi?"

"I sure am," she responds. "Though you really don't have to do this. I don't mind cooking something up here. There's no need to make a fuss."

"Oh, there's definitely a need to make a fuss. You're not cooking and cleaning on your birthday. We're taking you out. We've already been through this." I reach out my hand to her, and she takes it, pulling herself up.

"Well, okay, but I'm paying." She grabs her purse from the end table.

"Not a chance," Liam says, extending his arm.

Mimi slides her arm through his, and we head out.

"It sure is busy tonight," Mimi exclaims as we pull into the parking lot of one of the local restaurants, Blue's Joint. "Good for Blue."

Blue Becker is the man who owns this place. It's one of our favorite places to eat—that is, when we're not eating Mimi's cooking.

"Yeah, he's doing well for himself," Liam agrees.

Liam helps Mimi step down from the truck, and I shoot Emily a text. We walk toward the restaurant, which, from the outside, doesn't appear to be anything special—a run-down building in need of some updates and a couple of coats of paint. Yet all the locals know that there's no one in a thousand-mile radius who makes better barbeque than Blue.

We step inside, and as soon as we enter, a wave of, "Surprise," so loud that it almost pushes me back greets us.

Liam holds on to Mimi as she lets out a soft squeak of shock.

"Happy birthday, Mimi!" I laugh out, amused by the bewilderment on Mimi's face as she splays her hand over her chest.

"What is all this?" she wonders aloud.

"It's for you. It's your party," I tell her.

She looks at me with unshed tears. "It's too much, Leni girl," she states, just loud enough for Liam and me to hear.

I wrap my arms around Mimi and hug her tight. "It's not, Mimi. Not even close. You're very loved. Just enjoy tonight. You deserve it."

Almost everyone in town has made it out to celebrate Mimi. Westley and Emily with baby Sadie pull Mimi into a hug. Pete and Melody stand in line behind them. Mimi's friends from church, Liam's parents, and everyone else from the local postman to the car mechanic are here to shower Mimi with affection.

The space smells of the sweetness of barbeque and the saltiness of meat coming from the impressive buffet that Blue has set up on the back wall of the dining room. On the far side of the room is a large, throne-like chair with a pink crown resting on the seat, next to several tables holding all sorts of presents.

I collected photos from everyone in town for the past month, and I made a banner with large copies of all of the pictures acting as flags, attached to a thick twine that hangs in waves from the ceiling, like a garland of memories. All the images show how much Mimi has impacted Elkwood. Some of the photos show Mimi with her arm wrapped around someone in an embrace; others show her in the midst of laughter or with a smile. Many show people enjoying the food she's made for them over the years, like the one in front of me of a local farmer holding a cherry pie, his cast on display. To the right of the picture of the farmer is one of a woman holding her new baby, who's wrapped in a blanket knit by Mimi.

There were so many pictures given to me. It was amazing. Mimi had lost her husband way too soon, and unfortunately, she has a miserable son. She's always had me, though I was absent for the past several years, and I didn't show Mimi love as much as I should have. But, despite these shortcomings, she was never alone. She's the grandma to the kids without one or the extra grandma to the kids lucky enough to already have one. She's the sister, the daughter, or friend that one didn't realize they were even missing. She's the person in the community that can be counted on and is guaranteed to love you, no matter what.

Mimi's love is what makes her special. She has more to give than anyone I've ever met, and she shares it willingly. She's a gift, not only to me, but also to everyone in this community. She doesn't even realize it, which is why throwing her this party was so important to me.

I could never pay her back for loving me unconditionally when no one else did. I don't think I could've made it without her. I consider myself a strong person, but even the strongest need at least one person who loves them, unconditionally. What I wasn't given from my parents, I was blessed with from Mimi—tenfold.

I wrap my arms around Liam's waist, unable to wipe the wide smile off of my face as I watch Mimi talking to everyone.

"Thank you for helping me organize this," I tell Liam, who was a lifesaver in the planning of this party.

Like Mimi, he knows and is liked by everyone and is the reason that so many people showed up. He loves my grandma so much that he bought her farm for more than it was worth and insisted that she live there, which says as much about Liam as it does Mimi.

I'm so beyond blessed to be loved by Liam and Mimi that I have a hard time grasping just how fortunate I am.

Liam kisses the top of my head, his arm hugging me close to him. "Of course. Anytime."

We walk toward the large buffet.

"Hungry?" he asks.

"Starving," I reply.

"We need to make sure to steal your grandma away from her admirers in a few, so she can eat as well," he tells me as he scoops a big pile of mac and cheese onto his plate.

"Very true," I agree.

Mimi's gaze finds me from across the room, and the smile on her face is priceless. She shoots me a wink before reaching her arms out to hold another baby.

There was a while there when I was so miserable and nothing like Mimi. I was bitter, cruel, and pretty heartless, if I'm being honest. Yet Mimi loved me despite my shortcomings. I just hope, someday, that I can be half the person she is. She's taught me so much in my life, but I think the greatest lesson that I've learned from her is how to love.

"What a night." I lean against Liam's chest as we lie in his bed.

Everything about Mimi's party was perfect. She was so joyous and grateful. Most importantly, she felt loved, and that was the ultimate goal.

"It was. You did a great job." He lightly strokes his fingers up and down my back.

"We did a great job. You did at least half of the work." I chuckle.

"Are you happy?" he whispers, his voice slow as sleep starts to pull him in.

"The happiest."

"That's all that matters to me, Len," Liam says before his breathing slows, and his chest begins to rise and fall in slumber. He's finally given in to the much-needed rest he needs after the long workday that started before the sun came up this morning.

Most days, Liam falls asleep before I do, but usually, he works a hell of a lot harder than I do as well. It's something that I cherish though—this time of night. I love listening to the sounds of his sleep, his arm still around me, my skin still warm from his lips.

In these quiet moments each night, I reflect, giving gratitude to all the moments throughout the day that almost brought me to my knees with happiness. Lately, there've been a lot of them. More than anything, I'm thankful for Liam.

Growing up, I always feared that love would change me, turn me into someone I didn't want to be. There're many versions of love, and Liam has done nothing but love me in the way that makes me better. True love isn't selfish, belittling, or cruel; it's the opposite. It's all the ways in which Liam loves me.

Love is wanting someone to be happy and accepting them for who they are. It's not trying to force them into a mold that was never meant to hold them. Love is supporting their dreams, not telling them the ones they should have. Love is bringing them lunch when they're busy working. It's driving their grandma into town. It's holding their hand on long walks and kissing their lips as if they are your lifeline. It's bandaging their cuts and preventing new ones.

Liam loves me in a hundred different ways every single day, and all of them are just what I need to feel it.

I happened to find my soul mate when I was six, and I think a part of me always knew it. I just had to get to this point in my life to realize it.

As sleep pulls me under, I don't even wish for dreams because I live one every day with Liam by my side.

epilogue

Leni
One Year Later

I tightly wrap my arms around Liam's waist as we ride his black stallion, Jet, through the pasture. Resting my cheek against Liam's back, I gaze out toward the horizon where the oranges, purples, and pinks of the sunset are fading into each other like a beautiful watercolor painting.

This is my favorite part of the day on the ranch. After a day of hard work, the sky shines with serene beauty as the land falls to slumber. Our ride is always accompanied by the calming song of the birds singing and the crickets chirping and the warm winds of dusk.

It's magical.

Or maybe this is just what true happiness feels like. Perhaps everyone who's found their way on this journey we call life feels the same way as I do right now. I don't know though. Sometimes, I think that no one on earth could possibly be as happy as I am.

We put Jet away in the barn and walk hand in hand toward Mimi's house. We're greeted with strawberry rhubarb pie and vanilla ice cream.

"This is heaven, Mimi, per usual."

"So good," Liam chimes in through a mouthful of pie.

I can't help but laugh.

"What room are you all working on now?" Mimi asks in reference to the house that Liam's having built for us.

He's been involved in every aspect of the design, making sure his friend Pete creates the perfect floor plan.

"Leni's studio," Liam says proudly.

"Oh my gosh. It's amazing. It spans across the entire end of the second floor, and the walls are nothing but windows. So, I'm going to get the best light all day long. It's so great."

"That's wonderful. You need a good space to create. How many shows do you have lined up?" Mimi asks.

"So far, about ten over the next year."

I can't believe how well my art has been received. I can get into any art studio I want in Texas, and all the decent-sized cities have some incredible studios. My Texas-themed canvases are huge sellers. The great thing is, I only have to step outside my house, and there is inspiration everywhere. I feel like I'm exactly where I was always meant to be.

I get to spend my days with Liam and Mimi. I can help Liam on the ranch anytime I want, which is more often than I would've thought because the truth is that I miss him throughout the day. I can paint and create whenever I want as well, and I'm actually making really good money, selling my work.

Liam's parents spend quite a bit of time with us at Mimi's house, and I know Mimi's heart is full with joy. I'm happy I'm here. I'm so glad she's not alone. She actually has a large, extended family now, one that loves her.

I haven't spoken to my parents since walking out of my dad's hospital room over a year ago, and I'm actually okay with it. Now that I'm an adult, I get to choose my family, and I've chosen a pretty incredible one. I have no complaints. I've finally realized that I can't change them, but I can stop allowing them to affect the way I feel.

Forgiveness.

We help Mimi finish cleaning the kitchen before we say good night.

Stepping out onto the back porch, Liam threads his fingers through mine. "You ready, wife?"

"Ready, husband," I say with a snicker, still giddy over the fact that I'm now Mrs. Moore.

Liam and I got married a month ago at dusk below a candlelit archway in the field where we'd first met so many years ago. Only Mimi and his family were in attendance, and it was perfect. He'd offered me a grand wedding, but I had no interest in it. I've learned life lessons at warp speed during the time I've spent here since returning from New York. I no longer crave the acceptance of a couple of hundred people oohing and aahing over me in my wedding gown. That sort of affirmation from others isn't required anymore. I only desire it from one person, and he already thinks I'm the most beautiful woman in the world—even with bedhead and morning breath.

We walk the path from Mimi's house to our dream home. It isn't complete yet. It's still very much a construction zone, but it has the basics to live in, and it's ours. Liam stops on our front porch and swoops me up in his arms, causing me to laugh.

"You don't have to keep doing this!" I exclaim. "You've carried me over the threshold for a month now. I think we've made our point."

He doesn't listen as he walks me through the front door and sets me down. He takes my face in his hands and leans down until he's just a breath away. "I love it," he whispers, his voice husky and deep. "I still can't believe you're mine."

"Well, you'd better start believing it because I'm not going anywhere." I stare into his deep brown eyes, so full of love.

He kisses me, and it makes me feel amazing, like it does each and every time. I pray I never tire of kissing Liam. I don't know how I could. We're going to be those eighty-year-old grandparents who can't keep their hands off of each other.

He pulls his lips away. "Bath?"

"Yeah." I nod.

The kitchen, master bedroom, and bathroom are the only completely finished rooms in the house so far. But, honestly, that's all we need. We don't really use the kitchen since we eat with Mimi, so actually, we have more rooms than we require.

Liam runs the water in our huge claw-foot tub, adding in some lavender salts. We went all out on our master bedroom and bathroom. They could be straight from a magazine; they're absolutely stunning.

I remove my jeans, dropping them onto the tiles.

"Let me help you, Mrs. Moore."

Liam steps behind me and pulls up my T-shirt. I raise my arms as he removes it. He pulls down one of my bra straps and kisses my shoulder where the strap just was before repeating the motion on the other side. He sweeps my hair over one shoulder, and his soft lips trail across the back of my neck as his fingers lightly caress my arms.

I sigh in contentment.

He kisses down my back until he reaches my panties. He pulls down on them, and as they fall to the floor, he playfully bites my ass, causing me to jump.

"Hey," I say with a chuckle before stepping into the hot water.

Liam gets in behind me, and I lean back against his chest. I run the soapy sponge up and down our arms as we talk about our day. Liam and I never run out of things to talk about. He truly is my best friend.

"Are you and your dad running to Austin tomorrow?" I ask as I turn around to face him, straddling his lap.

"Yeah. Do you want to come?" His soapy hands find my breasts.

I close my eyes as his fingers focus on my nipples.

"Uh, no ..." My breaths come out harder. "I'm going to ... finish ... a few pieces ..."

He starts to rock against me, his hard desire hitting me right where I want it.

"For the show ... next week."

Liam moves one of his hands down under the water until he finds me. I drop my forehead against his chest, panting, as he pleasures me below the warm water.

"Oh ..." I moan.

"Does that feel good, baby?" Liam asks, his voice needy against my neck.

"Oh God ... yes." I rock harder against his hand. "I want ..."

"What do you want, Leni?" His fingers pick up their pace.

"I want ..." I moan.

"What, baby?" his hot breath whispers into my ear. He bites softly on my earlobe.

"You," I cry. "I want you, Liam."

He slides his hard length into me, and I plunge my body down onto it. Our mouths find each other, and we exchange sounds of ecstasy through our kisses. Liam wraps his arms around my back and holds me against him as our bodies move faster, both desperate to find our release.

Water splashes. Moans echo. Skin slaps.

Every time with Liam is the best time. Each time we come together, it's mind-blowingly good. Our minds, bodies, and souls were destined for one another.

After our bath, our bare bodies lie in our bed, snuggled up together under the blankets. We've yet to get the house wired for TV, so our evenings are spent talking and making love. I have zero complaints.

Liam holds me in his arms as the side of my face rests against his chest. I can hear his heartbeats, and I'm grateful for each one.

"I love married life," I sigh, my body humming with contentment.

"Me, too," he agrees, his fingers tracing light circles against my skin.

I prop my head up, so I can stare into his eyes. He's so gorgeous. In his face, I see the six-year-old boy I met so many years ago, full of curiosity, energy, and mischief. I also see my twenty-five-year-old husband—strong, steady, loving, and good.

"Are you happy?" I ask, already knowing his answer.

"The happiest." He grins and kisses the tip of my nose.

"Me, too." I smile back. "Thank you for loving me," I say.

This conversation is a regular one in our home.

"Always," he says, his answer the same as usual.

Every day, I have to remind myself that this life is real, and it's forever.

Liam's lips find mine, and I'm lost in his kisses once more.

Most of my life, I never thought I'd find this level of joy. The nagging feeling that it just wasn't in the cards for me was ever present. I spent years running and searching, trying to fill a void, when, in actuality, I'd always had everything I needed to be happy. I don't regret anything though. I think the journey was crucial for me to truly appreciate the destination.

The book has closed on the lost chapters of my life, the ones where I wandered aimlessly, searching for meaning. Now, I get to write a new story with Liam. He makes me feel more loved than I knew possible. I feel safe and accepted and so very cherished. Every day is a new adventure, full of laughs, love, and lots of kisses. We have so much to look forward to. We're just getting started. I can't wait to build a big, beautiful family with Liam, one in which our children will be loved unconditionally. We have years of pure bliss ahead of us, and I'm going to cherish every second of every minute of every day because I know how precious this life is. It's a gift I'll never take for granted.

#bestlifeever

epilogue

Liam
Six Years Later

Walking into my house, I'm met with an air of happiness and laughter. The four beautiful souls under this roof are all busily engaged in their activities, granting me with one of my favorite things in life—stolen moments where I get to observe, cherish, and give gratitude toward my blessings.

The main floor of our home is one open space, containing a dining area, huge living area, and kitchen. There are no walls to separate the areas in which we live and make memories as a family. It's a perfect design. It took Leni and me a couple of years from start to finish to get our dream home exactly the way we wanted it, but the end result was worth it. I couldn't ask for a better place to raise my family.

Leni sits on a chair opposite the window. A canvas rests on an easel in front of her, and a paintbrush is in her hand. To her side sits her mini me, our five-year-old daughter, Addie. Addie is so much like Leni; it's crazy. She has bright green eyes and deep chestnut hair that swings in a long ponytail, just like Leni's. She faces a canvas, a brush in her hand.

"What color should I make the sky, Mama?" she asks.

"What color do you want to make the sky, baby?" Leni answers.

"I don't know. You tell me," our little spitfire says to her mom.

Leni's head shakes. "I can't." She shrugs. "Art is very personal, baby girl, and there's no wrong way to do something. You paint what your heart tells you. Only you know what that is. What color would make you happy?"

"Pink," Addie answers.

"What kind of pink?"

"Light pink." Addie nods, determined.

"Oh, like the pink from the sunset last night?"

"Yes, that's what I was thinking!" Addie says. "That pink makes me happy."

Leni grabs a container of paint and pours a little bit into a dish on Addie's easel. "That pink makes me happy, too. Good choice."

Addie tilts her head up toward Leni and smiles, her expression filling with pride at her mom's approval. It makes my heart ache, seeing my wife with our kids. She's such a great mom, so patient, supportive, and loving. She's a better wife than I could have ever imagined, and yet, somehow, she's an even better mother. I'm so blessed to be able to share this life with her.

Our three-year-old Kellan sits on the counter of the kitchen island in just his underwear. His face and chest are splattered with white powder, which I know is flour.

He loves cooking with his Mimi and always ends up wearing more flour than what ends up in the bowl.

"Can we put chocolate chips in the muffins?" he asks his great-grandma. His eyes—also a bright green, just like his mama's—peer up to Mimi, hopeful.

"Well, of course, my love." Mimi taps him on the nose.

"Can I do it?" He reaches for the measuring cup in Mimi's hand.

"Okay. Hold it tight while I put them in."

He sticks out his tongue in concentration while Mimi pours the chips from the bag into the measuring container in his grasp.

"Is that enough, you think?" she questions, pouting out her lips.

"No! More!" He giggles.

She laughs and dumps even more chocolate into the cup. "There you go," she says as Kellan empties the chips into the batter.

He grabs the wooden spoon to stir, and it slips, accidentally flicking a wad of batter onto Mimi's chest, causing the two of them to break out in a fit of laughter.

Leni and Addie turn from their paintings to see what the commotion is all about.

Addie squeals when she sees me. "Daddy!"

She drops her paintbrush and runs toward me. I lift her into my arms and hold her tight before planting a kiss on her forehead.

"How's my baby girl?"

"Good. I'm painting with Mommy!"

"I saw that." I shoot my wife a grin. "You're both very talented."

"We're making muffins with chocolate chips!" Kellan exclaims in his little voice that no longer sounds like a

231

baby, but he still mispronounces some sounds. He's growing so fast.

"Awesome, buddy. I can't wait to eat them all." I take a step toward the counter, Addie still in my arms, and pinch his belly.

"No way. I'm going to eat them all!" Kellan grins.

"You have to share, Kellan," Addie corrects him, taking her big-sister role seriously.

Leni joins us at the counter, and my lips find hers.

"How's Mommy today?"

"Mommy is great. How's Daddy?" She kisses me again.

"Daddy is wonderful." I drop my hand and inconspicuously pinch her ass.

The two of us started calling each other Mommy and Daddy when Addie was a baby, trying to get her to say our names, and it kind of stuck—when we're in front of the kids at least.

I set Addie down, and she runs over to Mimi, asking to lick the spoon covered in batter.

"How's the baby?" I rub Leni's very large stomach.

"Still in there," she groans.

"He'll come out soon." I kiss her again.

She's still a week out from her due date, and considering our other two were each a week late, she knows chances are, she has a couple of weeks left. This pregnancy has been the most difficult, and she's ready to have it over with. I don't blame her.

"You're such a good mom," I tell her.

I'm so proud of the fact that not only is she carrying my son and keeping him safe for nine months, but she's also giving her all to the two she's already blessed me with. She amazes me every day.

"He's so happy in there. He doesn't want to come out."

"Oh, he's coming out, or I'm evicting him."

"I'll help you with that," I tell her quietly with a wink, not saying more at the risk of being absolutely inappropriate in front of her grandmother, but Leni knows what I'm referring to.

Her doctor said the best way to go into labor is to have lots of sex, and we have been—every night.

I walk around the island and give Mimi a kiss on the cheek. "How's my favorite Mimi in the whole world?"

"Good. I made one of your favorites for dinner tonight. Fried chicken and rice and gravy." She grins.

I hold my hand to my heart. "You're the best. Though, at some point, you really should teach this wife of mine how to cook. I feel like she takes advantage of you," I kid.

Leni scoffs in protest. "I do not. She loves cooking, and frankly, I suck at it. Right, Mimi?"

"I wouldn't say you suck at it, Leni girl. You just need more practice," Mimi answers.

"A lot more practice," Addie chimes in, already showcasing her sass that she inherited from her mom.

"Hey! You're supposed to be on my side."

"Mommy, your pancakes are always black." Addie scrunches up her face.

Leni rolls her eyes. "Well, that's because some people like them black."

"No one likes them black," Addie deadpans, and we all chuckle at Leni's expense.

"Well, good thing we have Mimi then, huh?" Leni says.

"Good thing!" Kellan says loudly.

"I have a surprise for you all," I tell my family. "Cassie is getting ready to have her baby."

Addie squeals, and Kellan claps.

"Can we see her?" Addie asks.

"Of course. We should go out now though, so we don't miss it."

"I'm going to clean up in here. I'll be out in a bit." Mimi says.

I would protest and insist that she take a break and tell her that we'll clean up, but that's a conversation I've had many times before with her, and I've never won. Mimi insists on helping out, more than she should. She cooks and cleans and truthfully loves to do it. She believes that, the second she stops working, she'll die. Who am I to argue with her? Love comes in all forms, and Mimi has always expressed hers this way.

I help Kellan wash up and throw some clothes on him, much to his disappointment, and we head outside. That boy would live in his underwear if we let him.

We make it to the barn just in time to see Cassie give birth.

Addie and Kellan are full of giggles and utter the occasional, "Ew, gross!" throughout the delivery, but the end result is always the same. Wonderment.

"I want to name her," Addie exclaims after we find out the calf is a girl.

"No, you named Princess Stardust," Kellan protests.

Leni nods. "You were the last one to name a calf, baby."

"Fine," Addie relents. "What are you going to name her?" she asks Kellan.

He stands on the wooden fence, looking in at the new baby, puckering his lips in thought. Finally, he nods once and states, "Chocolate Chip Muffin."

Addie curls her lip and looks at him, unsure.

"I like it. Very good name," Leni says.

"I agree. We can call her Muffins for short," I say.

"Yeah!" Kellan says. "Muffins."

The kids run around the barn while I make sure the new mama and calf are tended to. Leni props herself against the fence and watches me, her eyes dark.

"You look like you want to eat me for a snack." I chuckle.

"Oh, but I do." She suggestively raises her eyebrows.

I step toward her and press my lips against hers, tasting her sweetness. "Tonight, baby," I say against her lips, pulling her bottom one with my teeth, eliciting a sigh.

"Thank you for loving me," she says, serious now. "No one could love me better. I'm so lucky."

I hold her face in my hands. "I'm the lucky one, Len. Truly." I softly kiss her.

The new calf hesitantly waddles over toward the fence and sticks her head through. Addie and Kellan rush to greet her. Addie extends her pointer finger out, and the calf sucks on it, causing Addie to giggle loudly. I watch my firstborn with her big smile, green eyes, and chestnut hair. She looks just like Leni did when I first met her and laughs exactly like her mom did the first time a baby cow sucked on her finger. Life really has come full circle, and as I take in this incredible view before me, I know it was always destined to be this way.

There are countless paths to love, but for me, it all revolves around one—Leni.

acknowledgments

To my beta readers, blogger friends, author friends, and readers who message me—You all are so awesome. Seriously, each of you is a gift, and you have helped me in invaluable, different ways. I love you all so much. XOXO

This book especially wouldn't have been what it is without a few incredible women—Kylie, Amy, Gayla, Kim, and Tammi. Thank you so much for everything. I love you all very much and am so grateful for your love and support.

To the bloggers—I adore you! Out of the kindness of your hearts, so many of you have reached out and helped me promote my books. There are seriously great people in this blogger community, and I am humbled by your support. Truly, thank you! Because of you, indie authors get their stories out. Thank you for supporting all authors and the great stories they write.

Lastly, to the readers—I want to thank you so very much. Thank you for reading my stories and loving my words! I wouldn't be living this dream without you. Thank you from the bottom of my heart!

You can connect with me on several places, and I would love to hear from you.

Find me on Facebook:
www.facebook.com/EllieWadeAuthor

Find me on Instagram:
www.instagram.com/authorelliewade

Visit my website: www.elliewade.com

Remember, the greatest gift you can give an author is a review. If you feel so inclined, please leave a review on the various retailer sites. It doesn't have to be fancy. A couple of sentences would be awesome!

I could honestly write a whole book about everyone in this world I am thankful for. I am blessed in so many ways, and I am beyond grateful for this beautiful life. XOXO

Forever,

Ellie ♥

about the author

Ellie Wade resides in southeast Michigan with her husband, three young children, and four dogs. She has a master's in education from Eastern Michigan University, and she is a huge University of Michigan sports fan. She loves the beauty of her home state, especially the lakes and the gorgeous autumn weather. When she is not writing, she is reading, snuggling up with her kids, or spending time with family and friends. She loves traveling and exploring new places with her family.